Spiriting Through Christmas

CROWVUS

First Published in 2019

Crowvus, 53 Argyle Square, Wick, KW1 5AJ

ISBN: 978-1-913182-10-6

www.crowvus.com

Foreword

The short days and dark nights have returned and, even as I write this foreword, the veil between the world of the living and the world of the dead has thinned and blurred. We have celebrated Halloween and are moving through the season of memory and remembrance, with the weather reflecting the season: high winds, cold nights and bitter rain.

It's definitely a good time to snuggle up with a book.

So, we present our third ghost story anthology: Spiriting Through Christmas. We received so many excellent entries that our judges had a difficult time establishing a longlist, shortlist and, finally, choosing the top three entries.

Our book begins in a small village in East Yorkshire, where The Unexpected Ghost by Peter Collins takes place. The first place in our competition this year, this is a tale with twists and turns, playing on the stereotypes ghost stories have established to create a story which feels comfortable, light, yet chilling all at once, and a setting which is infinitely believable.

We are taken back in time with Maddie Wren's winning entry for the 11-16 Years category. December 1957 is a story which creates the atmosphere of the family home, with bewitching attention to detail. The First Rule by Tamsyn Sayles, the winner in the Under 11 Years category, shares emotions and beliefs in a way that is very impressive for such a young author.

For Knowing Linda, by Jan Steer, we are taken to rural Wales in a story which brings to life a place where the industry and happenings of the past are still left in more than just the memories of those still living. Muckle Flugga is a highly atmospheric story and Alison Weston transports the reader to the remote and wild island at the northernmost tip of the British Isles, where the supernatural is able to exist, untamed.

Cindy Xin's story J, which was Highly Commended in our Children's category, is a story which is chilling and heartrending in equal measure, telling the story of a girl who will do anything to care for her ailing father.

The significance of relationships is also explored by Natasha Davies in the darkly believable setting for It Could Have Been Me, which follows a survivor of domestic abuse.

Time and Tide, by Claire Marsh, is a classic ghost story which follows many of the guidelines that M.R. James set down for the creation of ghost stories: a contemporary setting and vengeful spirits, still unable to rest due to the manner of their deaths. We remain with a sea theme for The Watcher, our second story by Jan Steer and the third place overall in the competition. Here, guilt leads not to vengeance but to a sense of lost friendship, which is then rediscovered in through conversation and reassurance – a tragic yet heart-warming read.

An almost pantheistic story, which explores various species and leads the reader seamlessly into a murder mystery, Ampersand by Annabel Hynes reinvents the idea of what it means to be a ghost, and how helping even a person we never knew can give us back a sense of purpose we may have lost. We are taken back to the Victorian period, that classic setting for ghost stories, for Josephine Rummage's dark story, No Rest for Merry Gentlemen, which was the Runner-Up in the Children's category.

Bound for Eternity by Grace Dodridge is a terrifying and claustrophobic tale where an apparent stroke of good fortune leads to a dark discovery and a spine-chilling haunting. Kate Fleet's Top of the Stairs is a story which comes from a tragedy buried in the past and explores how important a sense of home is, even a long time after life is gone.

Our final Highly Commended entry from the Children's category, A Phantom Fair by Estrella Burgess, is a creepy, almost poetic, piece of writing, where a phantom is the herald of death. Second place overall was Papa Salvatore by Philip Gibson, a beautiful story within a story, sharing the great love between a father and his son. A truly heart-warming way to bring Spiriting Through Christmas to a touching conclusion.

Now turn the page and lose yourself in stories which will make you laugh, cry and shudder. The season for telling ghost stories is well and truly upon us – but these stories will entertain you all year round.

The Unexpected Ghost

by Peter Collins

(1ˢᵗ Place)

The guidebook called the walk a bracing climb leading to spectacular views of the East Yorkshire coastline. Somebody really needed to talk to that guidebook author. It should have said it was a knackering slog up a massively steep slope where there was too much mist to see anything. I sucked in a much-needed lungful of sea air and said a silent prayer of thanks as I came upon a welcome bench at the side of the footpath. Gratefully, I took off my rucksack and sat down and stared over the valley. I made a grudging apology to the author of the guidebook for the view at least. Through breaks in the mist I could see rolling green hills leading to a series of dramatic cliff tops that fell away to a spectacular shoreline where the waves crashed against the beaches. I could taste the sea air, and the warmth of the early summer sun was gentle and relaxing on my skin. I took out my water-bottle and frowned as I realised it was empty.

As I was wondering how to fill it, I was interrupted by a sudden noise behind me. I turned to see an old man staring at me. He looked about eighty, with gnarled weather-beaten features and wearing rough fisherman's clothes.

'Morning,' I said politely.

To my surprise, he spat on the floor at my feet before looking me aggressively in the eye.

'Another bloody ghost hunter, is it? Searching for the paranormal?' He raised a long bony arm and pointed at me. 'You need to show some respect.' He spat again and then turned and headed away from me along another footpath.

I was so taken aback by this strange interruption that I was momentarily lost for words. By the time I had gathered my thoughts sufficient to challenge him he had disappeared from sight. I followed the footpath which led away from the cliff to a nearby road. There was no sign of the old man in either direction. But on the other side of the road was a small teashop, The Copper Kettle. It was an old white-walled building with dark wooden beams. A large woman wearing an old-fashioned apron was sweeping leaves from the side of the building. I took the water bottle from my rucksack and crossed to speak to the woman.

She spoke without looking at me.

'It's not open, if that's what you're after. Not been open in years, this place. They used to pay me to keep it clean. But they don't pay me no more.' She continued sweeping with a strong, vigorous action and then looked accusingly up. 'But I can't just let it go to rack and ruin, can I? It wouldn't be right, would it?'

I mumbled my agreement. I sensed that she'd be of no help in locating the old man, so instead I politely held out my bottle. The woman pointed to the rear of the cafe.

'There's a tap out back. Help yourself. I'm done, anyhow.'

She planted her broom near the front door, picked up an old coat and bag and made her way slowly out.

I headed towards a small courtyard that backed on to what looked to be old stables at the rear of the café. As I entered, I felt a distinct chill despite the warm weather. I shivered uncomfortably. It was an eerie, unpleasant feeling, as if the chill was emanating from the very ground upon which I stood. I found the tap and filled my bottle. As I sat down, there was a sudden noise from one of the stables and I thought I heard somebody swear. Cautiously, I stood up and headed towards the noise.

'Hello. Anybody there?'

I pushed the stable door. The old hinge complained loudly as if it had not been moved for years. I stood still for a moment, the scent of dust and decay heavy in my nostrils. At first I could see nothing in the gloom, but as my eyes became used to the dark, I could make out an indistinct shape at the back of the stable.

'Ee, its breeght out theere, in't it.' It was an old-fashioned Yorkshire accent. 'It's all reet, tha can come in.'

I walked further into the room and saw a young man sitting on an old milking-stool. He was dressed in a dusty military uniform and was cleaning a long rifle. He got to his feet and extended a hand.

'Tommy Ackerman. Currently attached to the East Yorkshire Regiment.'

He smiled slightly as he spoke. We shook hands. Ackerman's hand had a cold, clammy feel as if some of the cleaning fluid had been spilt on it. I introduced myself.

'That's a grand get up, feller,' said the young man, indicating my fluorescent Gore- Tex jacket. 'What have you come as?'

'It's a walking jacket,' I replied rather self-consciously. 'So people can see me if I get lost.'

'They'll do all of that,' he smiled. 'I've never seen gear like it all my life. No one'll miss thee on a good day. Didn't need nowt special to go walking when I were a lad.' And he shook his head to himself.

I'd bought the jacket in a very expensive shop in Leeds as part of a new determination to get fit with my fiftieth birthday looming on the horizon. The sales assistant had assured me it was absolutely on trend, but I harboured my own private doubts.

'Isn't this an odd place to be cleaning your kit?' I asked, keen to change the subject. 'I've got stuff to learn.' His tone was downcast. 'And I never was the best scholar.'

He stood up. 'Here, you can test me.'

He stood to attention and then went through a series of manoeuvres with his rifle by his side, over his shoulder and then back down at attention.

'How was that?' He was slightly out of breath from his exertions.

'Very good.' Although I was not entirely sure what I had been looking at. I pointed at Ackerman's boot, where a long piece of cloth seemed to be unravelling itself.

'What's that?'

Ackerman bent down and began wrapping the cloth in place.

'Bloody puttee,' he answered. 'Most stupid piece of kit in the British army.'

He sat back down and began to clean his rifle again. I could see that it was very old- fashioned.

'Nice to meet you, mister,' he said, 'but if I don't get my kit cleaned, then I'll be on a charge.' He laughed moodily to himself. 'Got to clean your rifle, Tommy,' he muttered. 'Can't have it going off by accident again, can we?'

He continued muttering to himself and seemed to have forgotten my presence entirely. I nodded my goodbyes and left. Through some odd trick of the light, it was as if the young soldier had vanished back into the gloom.

I had just closed the door behind me when I felt it again; that strange and unnerving chill that seemed to rise from the courtyard floor. I shivered and emerged onto the pavement. Some sixth sense made me look up and I could see the old man who had accosted me earlier watching me openly from a bench across the road. I hesitated for a moment, but decided against further conversation with him. I headed back down the hill to the village of

Rennorth where I had booked a room for my walking weekend.

Although only a mile from the coast, Rennorth had the air of a quaint Dales village. The main street was still cobbled and most of the buildings were white-painted render with stone edgings. I had booked a room in the King's Arms for my walking weekend. It was a cosy old-fashioned place, with a welcoming fire burning in the grate even in the early summer. I ordered a pint at the bar and for a moment I considered asking the barman about the tea shop. But there was something about his expression that didn't invite conversation so I decided to keep my curiosity to myself. Instead I sat on a bench outside and put my phone's internet connection to the test. After a few false starts, I found the entry I was looking for under a website called Ghost Sightings in Yorkshire.

'The Copper Kettle,' it began, 'is an abandoned tea rooms on the East Yorkshire coast believed by many to be haunted. The café was a favourite of the soldiers of the East Yorkshire Regiment, and is largely unchanged from the time of its closure following a tragic killing in the courtyard.'

I paused for a moment. At least this explained the old man's outburst. I typed in 'puttee'. This generated the information that it was a sort of military legging equipment much in use in the First World War but which had ceased to be used by the 1940s. I changed the search again and typed in 'East Yorkshire Regiment.' The regiment had apparently been formed in the 17th century and disbanded in the 1950s. There were drawings and photographs of the regiment's uniforms for all those years. Tommy Ackerman had been wearing a First World War uniform. I tried to find out more about the killing at the tea rooms, but to my annoyance, there were no other entries, and repeated searches found little more of relevance. I was in contemplative mood when I went to bed that night. I considered myself a rational person, but the young soldier was definitely wearing a First World War uniform, and the old man's outburst hadn't been faked. Surely I hadn't really seen a ghost? But then I remembered that unnatural chill and I couldn't shake the feeling that something terrible had happened at the courtyard.

*

The following day was Rennorth Village Fete. Originally a highpoint of small village life, it had been kept on as a tourist attraction, and now brought a good number of visitors to the pubs, cafes and gift shops in the village. The highlight of the event was the village parade. I sat on a bench in the village square as a series of brightly coloured floats made their way past, with an announcer introducing each one. The sun was warm, and the village was busy with all visitors in the cramped streets. My mind was still preoccupied with the events of the previous evening and I was only half listening to the commentary. The voice over the tannoy seemed to drone on and on until one announcement made my ears prick up.

'Now, let's look at battles through the ages, with the history of the East Yorkshire Regiment.'

I looked up as the float came past. On the back were four young men dressed in army uniforms from different time periods. I stared at the third young man in the line-up. Boots, puttees, drab heavy uniform and long rifle. It was the man from The Copper Kettle. I stood up and stared. The young man caught my eye and waved.

'Ey up, mate. I've got it off pat now. What do you think?'

He raised his rifle to his arm and went through the same series of manoeuvres he had practiced yesterday. There was an ironic cheer from some portions of the crowd. I heard a women next to me chuckle.

'That Tommy Ackerman's a turn all right, isn't he?'

Her companion smiled in agreement. 'At least his rifle didn't go off this year.'

Feeling my cheeks redden, I turned away. Thank God I'd kept quiet in the pub. I felt in urgent need of refreshment and made my way back to the Kings Arms. I took my pint and sat on a bench outside reviewing the last 24 hours. How foolish had I been to even think I had seen a ghost? But even as I sat there, I knew I hadn't imagined that strange icy chill.

Something terrible had happened in that courtyard; but what?

My reverie was interrupted as somebody sat down on the bench beside me. I recognised him as the man who had accosted me yesterday. I nodded a curt greeting but the old man just looked at me for a while without saying anything. He took a long draught of beer and put down his glass.

'I had you wrong, lad, didn't I?'

'I'm sorry?'

'The Copper Kettle yesterday. It were you weren't it?' I nodded.

'I had you wrong. I thought you was out looking for ghosts but you wasn't, was you?'

I said nothing

'No. You wasn't looking for a ghost. But you saw one anyway.'

I felt myself blushing. 'I didn't see anything,' I said. 'I don't believe in ghosts.' The old man just sat there, his unblinking gaze on my face.

'I can always tell who's seen and who's telling stories. You've seen.' He took another drink and began his tale.

'It was 1958,' he said, 'and the Regiment was back at base for one last time.

Amalgamation, the army said, but as far as the lads were concerned, it was the end of the Regiment; the end of friendships that had lasted many years. They thought they would see it out in style with a major pub crawl. They took in all the pubs from here to Beverley. But one group made a mistake. Instead of calling at a pub, they called at a tea rooms. They stopped at The Copper Kettle.'

He paused for a moment and took a long pull at his beer. Despite myself, I found I was desperately waiting for him to continue. At length he took up the story again.

'The staff explained that it was a tea rooms with no beer. But one of the lads had had a bit too much to drink. He went into the courtyard and smashed a few glasses. The cleaner went out there and started sweeping up. The lad shouted at her to leave it, but she wouldn't listen. She just stood there sweeping away. The drunk lad kept saying she was disrespecting him, disrespecting the uniform, but she just ignored him. He tried to take the broom from her, but she was stronger than she looked and kept hold of it. In his rage he lashed out at her. She fell and hit her head on the paving in the courtyard. They say a cold wind rushed up through the ground and chilled everybody to the bone. She died there and then.'

The old man gazed in the distance for a moment and then returned to his tale.

'The place has been shut for many a year now. But the cleaner never went away. She stays there, sweeping away for all she's worth. But she'll never sweep away the memory of what happened there.'

He looked me straight in the eye. 'Oh you saw a ghost, boy. Just not the one you thought you saw.'

December 1957

by Maddie Wren

(Children's Winner 11-16 years)

Margaret Charles tied up her apron with a loose knot, then paused to admire it in the mirror – the floral design tastefully selected by her husband, George. She then checked the time on the grandfather clock in the hall, 8:30. He should be back in a few minutes, on the 8 o'clock train from London. She busied herself by checking on the roast lamb, the potatoes, the carrots browning in the oven. The time dragged on. She checked the clock once more, impatiently clicking her small heels against the polished floor. She turned on her Robinson radio, wincing at the sound of the static. Tuning into her favourite station, she sat, head tilted upwards, drinking in the sounds of laughter on the end of the radio.

Then she was overpowered by the scent of his aftershave. Sandalwood and citrus. She stood, straightening out her skirt and walked to the hall to greet him.

"I didn't hear you come in."

He cleaned his snow - clad brogues on the mat, slowly looking her up and down. "Is that the apron I got you?"

 She smiled at this remark, running her hands over the apron, "Yes, I'm worried about getting it dirty, even though that's its purpose!" She laughed and followed him as he strode into the drawing room, settling himself into one of their leather sofas.

"Gosh, you look ghastly. Would you like me to fetch you some whiskey to warm you up?" she inquired. He paused for a moment, looking mournful.

"Not tonight. I have my overcoat; I don't feel cold."

"I'm frozen. I fear it is as cold in here as it is out there." She gestured towards the window, which was rattling under the force of the gale.

"How was your day?" she asked, placing herself in the weathered armchair opposite him, folding one leg over the other with practised ease. He sighed, seemingly weary of the small talk.

"Like most other days, it was tiresome. I fired a young apprentice – he could barely tell his left from his right, let alone file my papers for me. I really could do without that nonsense now that

I'm getting old." He took off his overcoat with slow, strained movements.

"George," she tutted, "everyone's got to start somewhere. What's more, you are hardly getting old, I'd say you have got a few more years in you just yet." She laughed again. He didn't. Sensing the approaching silence, she excused herself to go and check on the lamb. As she turned her back on the Drawing Room, she heard him say something, quietly. She turned around to face him.

"What was that, George?"

He gave her a weak smile. "I do appreciate you Margaret."

"I know you do." And with that, she turned away to go to the kitchen.

She bent down, leaning into the oven. The potatoes were lightly roasted, and the lamb cooked rare, just as George liked it. She put on her oven gloves and placed the tray on the stove, listening to the chatter on the radio. She turned it up as she dished up the meal onto the blue porcelain plates.

'We are receiving information about a fatal accident on the 8 o'clock train from London, leaving no survivors. This train derailed near Potters Bar and crashed into…'

She turned the radio off.

Margaret paused. A deadly silence ensued, her hands hovering above her heart in a desperate attempt to still the rising panic. The 8 o'clock train.

"George?" She called out to him; her breathing quickened.

No reply.

"Did you take a different train?"

No reply.

She took hesitant steps towards the Drawing Room, waiting to see him there, the inquisitive eyes, framed by wrinkles.

The wind beat at the panes like two fists trying to shatter the glass. Cautiously, she entered the room.

It was empty.

No overcoat sprawled on the sofa. No dent in the cushions. No George.

Margaret cried out, crumpling onto the floor, head in hands.

She could smell his aftershave still. Sandalwood and citrus.

The First Rule

by Tamsyn Sayles

(Children's Winner – under 11 years)

My dress was as creased as the skin of a day old macaroni cheese, speckled with scarlet blood. The trees were towering over me, intimidating my matchstick legs running and tripping over the bed of twigs and the crisp blanket of leaves. Even if my heart was pounding like a professional boxer was cooped up inside- Even if my heart almost leapt out from underneath my skin- I couldn't stop – not now that I had got so far. I was trying to lose the worry, the anxiety stuck inside me- but it remained, laughing at my failing attempts to get rid of it. What if they found out the truth? The more I think about it, the more the cold snakes its way in through my purple lips. It feels like I am nothing more than a pure block of ice, the freezing water melting from the slightest breath of forgiving warmth. Panicking, I stumble over an arched tree root and my face is in the dirt, as crawling insects surround me. Crunch. Rustle. I try to jump to my feet, hoping, praying they hadn't found me.

A sleek, beige hare leapt gracefully out of the bush and reminded my muscles how to relax. I had to get up quickly before they caught me. I don't know what I've done wrong to THEM. Not really, anyways, I carry on through the chalky white mist. I strain to see a lone grave, with a raven perched on top the mist swirling around it. CAW! CAW! CAW! Its glossy black wings spread to fly, as a skinny figure appears and whispers to the gravestone "my child". I watch in silence. Her eyes are like the ocean on a summer's day- except they were obscured by swollen red eyelids, raw from crying, above her tear stained cheeks. My heart lurches with a horrid sense of guilt and I step forward and shout "Mum?" She turns, her eyes swivelling to the ground behind the jungle of twigs where I stood. Quickly, I pounced back behind the tree. "VIOLET?" I shove my fist into my mouth forcing myself to not to answer her continuous calls. Sighing she leaves. With my hands in my pockets I slump near the grave and read the name Violet Dane. As I look, my tummy churns like a stormy, dangerous sea. I lie on my back, looking up to the soft velvet sky of gleaming white, shining stars. It smelt of outdoors, life. How I missed life. Suddenly the glorious, earthy smell changed to stale blood and sweat. Before I knew it, a bony hand dangles over my head, holding a pair of metal handcuffs. They shout

"You're under arrest for murdering Violet Dane!!"

What? ….this is madness! I yell, the pain and anger flowing out. You're insane! All of you! I haven't killed anyone!! They looked at me with mixed expressions as if a signal that I was the one who lost my mind. I take my hand out of my pocket pulling out a delicate locket. To remind me. Just once. A man snatches it from me, opening the clasp to one side. "No" my voice cracks like the dyeing embers of a scorching fire. On one side of the locket is a photo of the lady who had been at the grave- except her wheat coloured hair was fair and wavy and a massive smile was painted across her pretty face- my mother- and the other side, it was me! The group turn the locket around deciphering the engraved name. "Violet Dane and Maria Dane."

I never used to believe in ghosts. Maybe that's because I am one.

My body fades and I feel as if someone's lifting me up, as though invisible hands are pushing me into Violet Dane's grave- my grave. No matter the struggle, I was trapped. I DID kill Violet- I committed suicide after years of stress and pressure. How clueless I was.

I watch the turf cover over my body and I'm stuck once more.

Is this where I belong? Is this my future? Lying in a rotting coffin and only aloud to escape on the 31st of October. The one night of freedom. The night you can look back into the past and see how much it has changed

So they didn't know the whole truth after all. Now they will never know. Who will ever tell them? Will this guilt stay with me for ever? I never had a twin. And if I did, I wasn't her. That is simply and scientifically WRONG.

Do humans really have no common sense anymore?

Pinned down like an insect under a microscope, I hear the chorus of confused words echo around me. "We watched her, we followed her and we caught her, we watched her disappear. Blimey, we've gone crazy!"

I never used to believe in unfinished stories.

I know now that that's the first rule of being a ghost.

Knowing Linda

by Jan Steer

The river had risen to its highest and so had the wind. It ran shrieking through the treetops, easily tearing the few remaining leaves from the twigs and flinging them, with great force, into a mad dance in the sky. The river, so swollen with icy water flowing from the mountains, had spewed the excess over its banks, onto the already sodden pasture, as Tom turned up the collar on his coat, pushed his face arrogantly into the wind and began his trek home.

The track, that ran between the tops of the fields and the base of the woods, was a treacherous place at this time of year. Always wet, always slippery and the thick, slate laden clay glued itself readily to his boots, slowing his pace. But he always walked this way. He enjoyed the loneliness and the quiet beauty of the cliffs that peeped insolently between the trees, wet and grey. The old slate quarries that had once employed so many, now hid in the woods, the thick boughs holding firm countless secrets against the stone faces. It was hard going trudging through the sludge and now the wind had begun throwing sharp needles of ice directly into his cheeks, making them tingle and sting. Tom rammed his hands deeper into his coat pockets and shivered on his way until a wet leaf slapped him hard on the forehead and cemented itself to his skin. Cursing softly, he extracted a hand to wipe it away. As he did so the pocket turned inside out ejecting his keys into the mass of rotting stems along the path's edge. Tom saw them fall and muttered obscenities as he bent to retrieve them. But, as his fingers began groping in the unfamiliar plants, a fiery pain shot, lance-like, into the back of his hand. "Damn it" he yelled into the gale. Quickly he spat onto the place and rubbed it into shiny moist circles on his skin. "Language!" chided a voice.

Startled, Tom leapt as if he had suddenly been touched with a cattle prod and he turned around sharply. There, just behind him on the track, stood a woman.

"Sorry. I thought I was alone." His voice was apologetic, but her one word had truly surprised him, for he had seen no one else on this journey. The woman said nothing but walked towards him and lifted his hand with her own.

"What's this then? Let me see."

"It's nothing really, just a nettle sting, I think."

"I think so too," she said calmly, at the same time her eyes knowingly searching the soggy undergrowth. "In which case we need a dock leaf."

"A what?" Tom queried.

"A dock leaf" she said again. "You rub it onto a nettle sting, and it stops the pain. Don't you know anything?" she asked, playfully mocking him in her sing-song, West Wales accent. Hurriedly, she found her leaf, spat on it and began rubbing it vigorously into the pink rash that was warming his skin. She spoke as she worked. "You're not local then?"

"No. From London originally. I moved here recently, just to get away from the rat race and to breathe" he answered.

"Ugh! I can't stand rats" said the woman and Tom guessed that she hadn't really understood him.

As she rubbed away gently with her slowly disintegrating leaf, he studied her. She was probably in her early twenties, he thought, and her blue-black, bobbed hair made an attractive frame for her clear-skinned face. Her eyes were large and pale blue the colour of the winter ice in the sun and they smiled up at him as she finished the job. "There we are then. That should do you, my boy." She shot the tattered leaf back into the grass.

Tom's hand felt better. "Thanks. I'm Tom by the way, Tom Hopkins."

The woman touched briefly at his hand. "And I'm Linda Evans. Very pleased to meet you Tom Hopkins."

They turned together and continued their journey side by side. He noticed that she was slim- built, clean and smart but surely her pale blue dress and navy-blue overcoat belonged to a different age? Women didn't dress like that anymore, not the women he knew anyway. Odd. Attractive but odd. But perhaps things were different out here in this wild part of Wales. This wasn't the city after all. Fashion mattered not one jot to the people living this far west. There was no one to impress here. She wasn't wearing tights though and he thought that strange given such grim weather. Then maybe she never felt the cold; some people just don't do they? Old leather boots encased her feet and, like his, they were heavy with the cloying clay, he noticed. She and Tom continued their journey together, periodically turning slightly to surreptitiously admire each other and chattering like happy sparrows. The noise of the violent wind had all but disappeared and although Tom did not notice it, the woods had suddenly grown eerily silent.

"Are you from the village?" Tom asked. "I've not seen you around."

"I used to live here," she said pointing towards a derelict cottage, "with my dad until he was killed in that quarry by there." She pointed to a tall, almost sheer, wall of slate just visible through the trees. "He slipped off the face. The slate followed him down and buried him."

Tom was shocked and as is usual with such revelations, he wasn't sure what he should say next. "Poor man. How awful for you. And your mother of course" he tried.

"Oh! Mam knew nothing about it. She lost her life giving me mine. I never knew her. It was always just me and dad."

He said nothing for a long while, keeping his thoughts private but feeling the pain of this beautiful young woman slicing through his insides like a cheese wire.

"I stayed on for a bit afterwards," she continued, "there was so much to do and besides I had my own position up at Forest Farm to consider. I was their maid; there were no daughters to help them up there, you see. She turned away from him and toyed with a coat button. "I loved the little ponies they kept there," she said wistfully. "Poor little dears. They didn't have much to look forward to in life, I don't suppose, but they had a good time while they were with us."

"I'm a bit confused," said Tom frowning, the lines on his forehead cutting deep furrows in his wet skin. "When was this? I thought that the farm had been empty for years. The place is dropping to bits."

"No, not years," said Linda wistfully and still twirling her coat button.

"But I was told that the quarries had packed in long before the war." It was as much a question as a statement.

"No, father fought in France and came here to live afterwards. I wasn't born until after the war, you silly boy." Linda was laughing, her straight, white teeth dancing attractively on her tongue as she did so. But Tom couldn't piece things together properly. If she had indeed been born just after the war, it would make her roughly the same age as him - which she wasn't. It made no sense at all but there was something compelling about her laughter, something infectious and Tom was happy just to laugh with her and dismiss the nonsense filling his head.

By now they were at the end of the track and at the old wooden stile that straddled the border between the trees and the lane. Linda stopped abruptly. Tom gripped the top of her arm ready to help her over, but Linda was immovable.

"You're not going on into the village?"

"No," she murmured, "not to the village; I'm going home."

Tom knew then why she was here. She was revisiting her old home and remembering old times. She could have picked a better day, he thought, but that was her business after all and none of his.

"Right, well I'll go on then. Thanks for the dock leaf. Good talking to you." He climbed the stile, chuckling as his boots slipped on the wet wood.

"I'll be seeing you again Tom Hopkins, soon." Her silken voice now sounded thin, weak and her image appeared oddly unstable in the failing light.. Tom shook his head, moving it in quick jerking movements, trying desperately to clear his vision, to re- focus. He felt strange. He must be coming down with a chill, he imagined. Not surprising, really, considering the interminable foul weather.

As he stepped out into the lane, the full force of the gale was again unleashed, and the ferocious wind tore into him. He looked back over the stile, but Linda had gone.

Then, burying his head deeply between his hunched shoulders, he began to battle his way down the lane, narrowing his body against the stinging, almost horizontal sleet, as he headed towards the village and home.

Later, feeling warm and dry at last, Tom lazed in a comfortable chair, toasting his toes in front of his log burner, sipping at his single malt whisky and thinking about the enigmatic woman he had met earlier out in the woods.

He was certain that he had not seen her before. She was shockingly beautiful. Had they met previously he would have remembered the moment without a doubt.

Tom spent an uncomfortable night in his bed. It was difficult to sleep with the noise of the undiminished gale howling in his ears and battering him into bouts of wakefulness. In the brief periods when sleep did find him, Linda appeared in his head.

When he awoke, her face was still with him and the vision stayed with him as he shaved, bathed, dressed and ate his breakfast.

Today was Saturday. The wind and rain had stopped at last and Tom pulled on his Wellington boots ready to head back up the lane and into the woods. Curiosity drove him to see if Linda would be there. Common sense told him that she would not. He had to check. The compulsion was too great to ignore.

"You're in a hurry today then," trilled a frail voice. It was Cecil.

Now in his eighties, he had spent all his life in the village except for a brief spell with Monty, in the North African desert, during the war. He was well wrapped up against the chill air and a woollen hat, with a pom-pom, covered his snow-white hair. Old age had finally found him and now he always took his stick with him on his slow, methodical walks up the lane and back. Tom liked walking with Cecil. He was very knowledgeable about everything concerning the village and its long history and he loved nothing better than to talk about the old days whenever the chance presented.

They walked together slowly, with Cecil gripping Tom's upper arm, for a little added support.

"I'm hoping to meet the girl I met yesterday," Tom began "we met in the woods when I was on my way home. You know that little ruined cottage by the end quarry?"

Cecil nodded. "Well, she said that it had been her home."

Cecil stopped, straightened up and scratched with a bony finger at his skull through his hat. "That can't be right Tom. Nobody has lived up there since the thirties. The chap that did live there had a daughter, really pretty girl as I remember, but he had an accident in the quarry. Lots of 'em did, mind you. Anyway, one day he took a tumble from the rock face and was crushed to death when the slate slid down on top of him.

No Health and Safety back then, of course. Nasty business. That would be about, let me see…thirty-five I should think."

A sudden feeling of uneasiness spread throughout Tom's body and he pressed Cecil for more information. He could not leave the story there.

"What about the girl? What do you know about the girl?" he asked excitedly.

Cecil thought hard and pulled at his chin. "If I remember correctly, she worked up at Forest Farm as a maid, or a servant, or something. The boys up there were always chasing after her that I do remember. My, she was a pretty one though. Anyway, when her father was killed, she never really got over it. Went a bit round the twist I think."

Tom's mouth had begun to dry. This had to be the girl he had met yesterday in the woods. But how could it be possible? Cecil was talking about her. It had to be her. Although every morsel of common sense argued against it.

"Do you remember her name, Cecil? This girl, was she called Linda perhaps?" Cecil looked off into the distance, trying hard to drag forward the distant memories, but he was finding it difficult.

"No, I don't think so. Mind you, my memory is not what it was. I think the family name was Evans. The girl lived on in the cottage for a couple of years or so afterwards, but she was found one day, face down in the water, in a cattle trough up at the farm, as dead as anything. Poof! Gone just like that." He clicked his fingers. "Nobody knew whether she had done herself in or not. There was some talk at the time that one of the farm boys might have had a hand in it. Someone who couldn't get his way with her perhaps, but I don't remember all of it now, it's too long ago.

Anyway, if you're interested, she is buried up at Saint Non's church, over by the railings, behind the old Ogham stone. Pretty girl mind. I can picture her now: thick, black hair and always in her blue coat come rain or shine." Cecil wiped his eyes. The recollection had affected him, but no the wind had made them run he said. "Those were the days young Tom. Ha! Those were the days."

Tom's face emptied to white and he said not one word more.

"You all right?" asked Cecil with genuine concern. "You look like you've seen a ghost."

"You know, I think I might have." The words were half whispered. "Just one more thing Cecil. Did they have lots of small ponies up at Forest Farm, can you remember?"

Cecil brightened. "Small ponies? I should say so. They had loads of 'em up at the farm. They used to buy them up regular as clockwork and then sell them on to the pits down in South Wales."

Tom spoke only to himself. "So that's what she was talking about."

Cecil was still talking. "Course the family fell on hard times; I don't know all of it exactly, but at the end of the war all the land was sold off and no one was living up there. The place has been falling to bits ever since. Damned shame really."

Tom never went into the woods that day nor for several days afterwards. He now knew the identity of the girl and far from feeling in any way frightened by her presence in that damp, forbidding place, he felt privileged to have met her.

***

The first frost had arrived early this year and its crystal rosettes lingered throughout the day on the headstones and the ornate wrought ironwork in the churchyard. Tom had arrived early for the Sunday service. With all that he had learned of Linda on his mind, he had headed directly for the Ogham stone and her grave. It was exactly as Cecil had said. The headstone was set up against the railings. Tom knelt down to read the inscription on it, pulling away the blackberry stems of this year's encroaching growth as he did so.

In Loving Memory Of

Sian Linda Evans

Who departed this life Nov.11th 1938 aged 20.

Only child of George Tudor Evans and his wife
Bethan Sian Evans

There was a short religious text, written in Welsh, beneath the inscription. Some china flowers sat under a glass dome amongst the grass growing over the grave.

Tom made to stand up as the church bell began its methodical calling of the faithful to prayer. The congregation had begun arriving. As he rose a nettle briefly kissed his hand piercing his skin with its stinging barb. He rubbed vigorously at the place swearing quietly to himself as a rash began to appear.

"You'll need a dock leaf for that" said a quiet, female voice. Tom spun around, shocked by the sound of a voice that he felt sure he recognised. This was the voice of Linda, the woman he had met in the woods, the woman lying in the grave at his feet. But surely that wasn't possible, was it?

"Look! There's one," said the woman pointing.

Tom tore it from the plant and briskly rubbed onto the back of his hand. She was slender, about twenty-five he noticed, and wearing a navy-blue coat buttoned all the way up against the cold. Her black hair was cut into a very neat bob and Tom stared at her, incapable of looking away just then.

"I'm Tom Hopkins" he ventured tentatively.

She said nothing but her eyes sparkled out, pale and blue, capturing his and holding them in her gaze as they stood close together in the still, cold air of the churchyard. "It's nice to meet you Tom. I'm Linda, Linda Evans." She held out a gloved hand. "I know," he said aware that he sounded ludicrous.

"What?" she quizzed.

"Look. I know that this is going to sound completely bonkers, but haven't we met before? I'm sure I know you from somewhere."

Linda screwed up her eyes and grinned at him impishly. "If that's a chat up line it's hardly very original is it?" This remark threw him off balance completely and aware of its effect, she moved closer to him and patted his arm reassuringly.

"I'm only teasing. I don't think we could've met though because I've only just moved here. I'm a Cardiff girl originally." She looked around and realised that they were alone.

"Look Tom, would you mind if I sat with you inside? You see, I don't really know anyone yet and I'll feel such a fool sitting there all by myself."

"Of course; why not?" he answered. "It will give the village something to talk about I expect" he whispered. They giggled as they walked into the church together and sat down in a pew.

Had they looked back as they left church that day, they would have noticed that curiously, the frost had now melted on Linda's grave and that the snowdrops growing around the headstone were already in bloom. But they only saw each other and never looked back.

Muckle Flugga

by Alison Weston

"Then, water-kelpies haunt the foord,
By your direction,
And 'nighted trav'llers are allur'd,
To their destruction…"

- Robert Burns

There is no fog, nor night so dark, nor storm so fierce that its piercing light cannot save.

Once he had thought the lighthouse would save him. That he could stop anyone else, suffering as he has suffered. If he could bring it here, imprison it here, then he could save more than just the ships, barely aware of Shetland's shores. There is no place more remote than the Isle of Unst, none so isolated as the Lighthouse at Muckle Flugga. For decades it has worked, but nothing is infallible and everything must break. The world stops as he sees it wrenching free, the storm smashing its brittle fetters.

Spiral stairs are slick with ocean spray, the cold seeps into his remaining hand, fingers first, carving claws from flesh. Disorientation sways weak knees, almost tilting forwards, catching the rope in the crook of his elbow. Whatever happens he can't allow it to escape. Air aches in his lungs, desperation pushing him downwards. Light, dark, light, dark. Thunder cleaves the clouds, resonating through his chest. White walls illuminate, lightning bright, and almost blinding. Beyond the door the ocean roars, venting frustration upon the shore.

It waits, bridle shattered against snarled rocks, free at last. It will finish what it has started.

Above him, the tower looms, casting out its warning. How many lives have been saved by this place? This unforgiving strip of land, hewn from the sea. Now it will be his grave, he knows it as surely as he knows the beat of his own heart.

Why has he brought it here?

Breath freezes in his mouth, fingers tremble against the handle. Once he had been a brave man. Now he is old, each winter claims more of him. Cold seeps into his joints, takes up residence there, until there is little room for movement. Slowly he is disintegrating. Iron is the same, time has worn it down, it has given way now. Here. There is scant hope of recapturing it, yet he must open the door. Even if it kills him this time, he must face it again.

Through driving rain he feels its eyes, luminous in dark relief. The sea has reclaimed it, weeds tangle through its mane. He has fooled himself, forgotten what manner of creature has shared his land.

Forgotten what he has trapped here. Now it hungers.

Scree is ice, his feet falter and it is over, before it even begins. The sound it makes stirs the hairs of his nape; unearthly, booming deep from it's chasms. It churns with anger as lips pull back and fangs snap the air. Hooves fly at his head and his hand stretches up to protect himself, an involuntary movement and a fatal error.

Flesh gives way as his hand grazes it's withers, sinking in to its corporeal form. It binds him. What once was fur, now is tar, enveloping him from fingertips to elbow joint. There is all the time in the world now, so they stand, centred in the storm for a moment of intimacy before the beast turns its head towards the waves that once had birthed it. Heels dig into the rocks, seeking purchase. A wild swing of his stump, a final Hail Mary, trying to grab at the iron chain that had bound it here.

Instead he feels the lurch of momentum, the steady gait that drags him inexorably down towards the seething, black abyss. Unable to look, his eyes instead fix instead where his hand once was. What it has cost him, what he has lost. There is no knife now, no chance to sever bones and sinew, just the steady pound of hooves.

Water fills him, seeks out those places where air belongs. It's not the cold, or the dread that consumes his final thoughts. It's the shaft of light, skimming water.

Light, dark, light, dark. Dark. Dark. Dark.

--

Oars heave, the roll of swell unsettling the cargo braced between his knees. Crazy old man. For as long as he could recall Muckle Flugga had been Dougal's land. Half of Unst had turned out the day he'd fetched up the pony. Eyes rolling with wild fright as it was winched up the Blondin cable. Folk said his wife had slipped into the sea one night. Folk thought that was what he was doing up there, looking for her.

There seemed some truth in it; only a man driven beyond his wits would eek out an existence on the edge of the isles. Dougal had taken the lighthouse and he had lived across the stretch of water, sheltered in shore. By rights he should have spent half his time at the lighthouse, but Dougal never wanted to leave, not matter how many times he had offered to take a shift.

The storm had been the worst in decades, even weathered as he was; Archie had huddled like a small child in his bed, as the wind had howled between the shingles. Only the familiar flare of the lighthouse had been a comfort, until he had counted 20 and light had not returned to the shore house.

It had taken hours for the sea to calm enough for Archie to cross, stomach sinking as no withered face greeted him as he wound the rope about the mooring. The climb to the lighthouse was steep, with each step the task ahead drawing closer. It had always been at the back of his mind, that one day he'd have to fetch the old man down. Whether a blessed relief or not, he cannot find the body. The land is scoured clean, any sign of Dougal removed, even the poor pony he kept for company.

The task is a grim one, alone in the growing dusk as he fits the new lamp. Every shadow fills him with dread, he can't work quickly enough, his touch is not deft. By the time he is done the water is polished obsidian, only the light of the moon remains, interspersed by the sweep of the lighthouse's beam. Archie cannot remember a longer crossing, though his oars cut through the stillness and his lungs are bellows. Relief warms him as sand rises up to meet his bow, splashing the last few feet to solid ground and the safety of the shore.

It's then he sees it, silhouetted in starlight, glistening in silver. It is the most beautiful horse he has ever seen. Conjured, as though from some tale of old; of knights and noble steeds. If only he can catch it he will be a rich man. Gaidhlig lilts, lullaby soft.

"Here boy, come here." And it does.

J

by Cindy Xin

(Children's Highly Commended)

Calculus puts up a long fight. Two whole minutes of hesitant convolvulation before the last of its pages die imperceptibly into the flames. I stalk the smoke from every angle, scouring for wisps that look remotely like a face, a leg, or an arm, but all to no avail. Of course it wasn't enough. He'd seen this trick before. He's tired of it. I fumble for a bucket hidden behind me, dip it into the stream, and put the fire out.

What an idiot move. You're not the same girl you were before and he knows it. What was a textbook gone for me now? Not even the barest sacrifice. Before it would've been the world. A fine slip I would have to add to my bills, a B on an assignment or two, humiliation. But now, it doesn't mean anything. I would have to do better tomorrow.

The walk home from the ravine is always a polarized experience. If J came, I would cross the three miles of hills, cars, and poverty in an easy hour. If J hadn't come, I'd spend two hours on the verge of tears, contemplating my wrongs. Today, J hadn't come. I had failed.

This evening, the usual San Francisco lights muddied with the Christmas lights over the Bay, dyeing it a color that made me sick. Cars passed slower in winter rain and the only people on the sidewalks were the people who had to be: chinese grocers carting fruits into and out of leaky stores, construction workers grouping together beneath unfinished roofs and teenagers running in the rain just because they could.

My thoughts raced faster than the wind. What would it matter I flunked out of another class or two? I wasn't the Lisa that wasted eighth grade studying to get into Longwell High anymore. I wasn't that shallow; I had moved on. A textbook was no longer an adequate sacrifice. I knew it and J knew it too.

—

My father takes up more than half of their house by his mere presence. Though he's thin, frail, and doesn't have the habit of cluttering, whenever he's around, I feel as if I'm confined to a space as wide as a desk.

He's where he's expected to be: on the couch, one arm crossed onto his face, the other one dangling an empty carton of soymilk off the edge of the seat.

I once took for granted how much spare time I had while her father was still semi-functional. A little too dependent on alcohol, but still healthy and working for an associates at the local community college. A little too religious and a little too dependent on others, but still capable of cooking dinner once or twice a week, or at least putting his clothes in the hamper once they were dirty. Back then, I could be who I wanted to be. Longwell Lisa. I could come home after eight, buy clothes for myself with my job at the grocers. Life wasn't glamorous, but it was still moving. I had more to lose. More things to offer J.

Though my father was a burden and though there was no other to put it, last Christmas, I still loved him and had worked overtime for a year to buy him a dingy, old TV with a crank that could continue playing Chinese soaps even when the power stopped, which it often did. After I bought it, my father had clapped his hands together childishly, stood up, opened the window, and yelled "I'M COMING HOME" into the cold, sterile air. After that, he took a walk around the apartment complex, smiling and waving at every other resident he crossed paths with.

I had been saving again this year for Christmas to buy him something better: a plane ticket. There were little things here and there that indicated that this would be the best way out for him. There was the TV, for one, whose Chinese folk tales could lull him even in his worst night fits, where he'd scream and cry for my mother and tear the armpits of his shirts out. There was also the time I had bought a new brand of pickled cabbage and watched as he galloped in ecstasy as soon as a piece had grazed his tongue. ("It's the taste of home!" he exclaimed).

I mindlessly cut up some bok choy, carrots, and whatever meat there was still left in their freezer and throw them into a soup. I leave a bowl by the coffee table, adjust Dad's blanket, and head out to work.

—

The day I met J, everyone at Longwell had already heard what had happened with George. That day, no one spoke to me but Annalise, my academic nemesis, who jealously reassured me that I'd be able to exploit the situation for my college apps when time came around. My teachers sympathetically never called on me in class. When I saw George in the halls, he just looked away. Earlier that morning, Dad revealed that he had officially dropped out to become a street preacher, the milk in the fridge had gone sour, and no light would open no matter how many times I flicked the switch. I was tired and angry and out of ideas.

That afternoon, I gathered all traces of George and headed down to the ravine, where our family used to have bonfires while things were still okay, to burn them. Letting go of George was not easy. From time to time, I'd dream of him again. How he made me and all the other girls feel. How he made all the boys jealous. How he smelled like sweet cumin and winter rain.

As soon as the flames swallowed the box, J was standing right in front of me. J, a body stitched from smoke. J, an ounce of wind scrimmaged into two warm palms. He was tall, his feet stood a foot over the ground. His veins protruded along his neck and forehead in a light bruised shade of pink. His eyes, brown and hollow, sank deeply and beautifully into his skull. He was barefoot and wore an untucked brown dress shirt and old gray khakis.

"Lisa? I've been waiting to meet you. I know your pain and your sorrow. I'm J. I'm not here anymore, but I'm here for you." His voice was so quiet it could've been wind.

——

Through the rain, I roll a cart of oranges into the store, my silhouette forgettable against the lanterns' quiet dim. J's absence still heavy within me, I let a few roll off the cart and onto the pavement. Mrs. Qiu, my fat and cheerful coworker who's chronically covered with duck grease, picks them up after me, humming a Christmas song she heard a Loawai sing.

Before J, there was Mrs. Qiu. She had been there for me since the incident with George last year. She called the clinic, shooed away the Longwell kids that would stare for a little too long, and helped me come to terms that no boy would ever want to touch me again. I swear I'll repay her someday.

She watches as I roll the cart in.

"Lisa, I told you already: even though if you need some extra money to buy your dad his Christmas present, I'm more than willing to give it to you."

"No, Ms. Qiu, I'm fine. It's not any work at all hauling around some oranges." She passes me a twenty. I pass it back.

"I can't take this," I say, though I want to. Twenty dollars is twenty closer to the tickets. Twenty dollars is two hours off overtime. Enough time to go to the ravine tomorrow. Enough time to try to summon J.

—

After the last of George had burnt away, J stuck around for weeks. Whenever I had trouble, he was there.

I confided in him about grades, girls, and work. I grumbled about cooking and cleaning for Dad and my worries of being tethered to Chinatown for the rest of my life. And he could see me. Like really see me. After Longwell had forgotten me and George in the bustle of test scores, extracurriculars, and unfriendly competition, I became friends with Anna and Delia, bookish quiet girls that came from the hills, who were too awkward to be pretentious. And though we could laugh together and though they knew about my struggles, they didn't really see me. They always gave the ritualistic Sorry's and the back-pats and the It'll get better soon's, but deep down I knew they didn't care.

But J did. He always did.

He had devoted his past life to people like me. After several visits to the ravine, I had pieced together his story. Arriving as an immigrant in the 50's, J had been searching for a strong community and was appalled by the options that were available. He found every previous spiritual movement corrupt and vowed to reform the way humans functioned in the world. In the 60's, he started a small spiritual group in Chinatown that combined Buddhism, Daoism, and Christianity and preached tolerance, asceticism, and most importantly purity. Those who were struggling in their hearts would visit him and he would tell them what to remember and what to forget. Savings— throw those away. Children— life will sort itself out for them, let them run free. Old photos and mailing addresses— they are only the poison that induce dissatisfaction. Only after all these things are gone will you be satisfied. According to J, after a woman had been freed, she left her family to live in the ravine with him and several others. Her husband, shocked, betrayed, and most importantly, unpurified, shot J in a fit of rage and self-righteousness.

 J called me his fallen angel and told me he could save me and Dad from our horrible lives. He said he could heal scars, physical and emotional. Whatever disease Dad had, I knew I wanted it gone. Whatever disease I had, I knew I wanted it gone too.

—

I find the pictures beneath the couch mats, scattered between coins and bills, which I add up to be exactly $2.23.

In them, I am innocent once again. An almost anonymous lump of pink lodged in between

Father's chest and his forearms. Though I haven't seen them in a while, there's some comfort knowing they still exist, that they ever happened. In one of them, Mom, Dad, and I are at Bellevue Park and it's Christmastime just like it is now. Mom is wearing her qipao, Dad is sporting a Santa hat and the San Francisco Christmas Lights are quiet enough to be beautiful.

I rub the photos against each other, a feeble attempt to warm my hands. The ravine's chill bites, but I start the fire and watch everything else disappear.

—

The first things J had me burn were my textbooks. I was ranked third in a class of seven hundred at the most prestigious school in SF. I had been nurturing this ticket out for as long as I could remember.

I said no, but things were getting rough. I stopped by the ravine and J wasn't there. Dad started throwing up blood, stopped leaving the house, and stopped reading the Bible. My grades were high, but were growing to feel increasingly insignificant to me. I thought more about J and what he had to say. I wanted to become purified more than becoming valedictorian.

As I watched my textbooks immolate, J appeared again, leaning stiffly against a tree.

You needed to let this go, he said.

Another time when he had disappeared, I cut my hair to my ears. I went down to the ravine and threw the whole bundle in the fire. After months of wishing just one boy would look at me, I watched my vanity flicker briefly then completely crumble into flames. When he arrived, J told me I was getting closer, but that I was still too far away.

Like a baby finally crawling. You'll learn to walk someday.

—

As the last of my baby photos convulse away in the flame, J still doesn't appear. I realize my mistakes: I felt strongly about the photos and I felt like it was a sacrifice to let them go, but they played no part in my goals anymore. Anchors of the past, they'd burn away and life would go on the same because it had to. No worries. No sacrifice. No purification.

 Tonight during dinner, I watch soaps with Dad, but can't concentrate when he speaks to me. I nod the entirety of two episodes and leave for work when the time comes.

"BE SAFE!" Dad yells childishly. "STEAL ME A PEPPERMINT CANDY IF YOU CAN! That stuff is good." "Okay, Dad."

———

Three days from Christmas, Dad makes congee for breakfast. He smiles as I wipe his nosebleed, raves about a news report that came from his hometown announcing the re-construction of his old school.

"It's just that that old creaky thing hadn't been safe enough to play on since I was a child. You never got the chance to go on and my little brothers didn't either. Now, the new generation will be able to have fun like I did! The world is fixing itself up again!"

I'm eight hours away from the tickets. Four more hours tomorrow and four more hours on Christmas Eve. While Dad hums "Jingle Bells" and "Last Christmas" mindlessly, sucking on peppermint and lychee candies I picked up for him from work, I flip through my bedroom looking for something else to offer J, but don't find anything.

———

J had always said I had too much pride, too much of the wrong kind of integrity. You care too much about helping others fulfill their evils as long as they think you're a good person. You don't need anyone but me to think you're a good person.

On Christmas Eve, Mrs. Qiu leaves her wallet in a storage closet. I pick it up to return it to her, but remember J's voice again.

In order to be saved, you need to rid yourself of worldly virtue.

At the end of my shift, I smile at Mrs. Qiu as usual, consoling her with the expected "you'll find it eventually" and leave into the dark as soon as possible. She had two children in high school and an old ailing husband, but I reasoned that money was worth as much as you made it and that the Qiu's didn't make much out of it. What was what was in her wallet worth anyway? Another night at the club for Mr. Qiu? Another pack of cigarettes for her son? Its disappearance would be a favor.

As the manager hands me this week's pay, I step into the dark. I think about Mrs. Qiu's money and her family. I think about Dad, what sacrifice and virtue truly are.

—

I count my money. $455.23. Twenty dollars and twenty-three cents more than what I needed to buy Dad his ticket. I put it in an envelope and write across its surface "FOR GOING BACK HOME!"

in the neatest handwriting though I've ever written in, though I know where it'll end up tonight.

The walk to the ravine feels the same, even at midnight. Cars roar anonymously down Route 480, indifferentiable in the flurry of headlights. The wind is a lonely friend biting the skin for attention and the stars are indecipherable beneath all the light pollution.

The last time I saw J he told me I was playing life too safe. That if my sacrifices meant anything, they would really hurt.

I gather the logs, light the fire and soak the wallet's low quality faux leather with my sweat. I stare at Ms. Qiu's brown-stained drivers license then the envelope that sat heavy in my palms. Slowly, I lay them on the dirt beside me.

In a couple hours, the San Francisco fog will rise and children will awaken to piles of presents and the smiling faces of those who love them. They will be held tight and for at least one day, they'll believe they hold the world. The folks on the hill will awaken to parties with friends they haven't seen in months, hold hands with each other to holiday jingles. The kids at Longwell will drive to their grandparents' house, forgetting about college apps and homework deadlines. My friends in Chinatown will awaken to a day when they can dream again.

Dad had always told me that I was the best child he could ask for. Obedient and calm yet determined. That once, I had successfully broken into a locked cabinet for a jar of cookies that I would later share with other neighbourhood children.

"We were all so surprised," he said. "You were the best child there. Never once even looking at that cabinet! But then BOOM, you got it all figured out!"

I want Dad to know that I'll get it all figured out again, all this crazy stuff in our lives. I'll purify the shit out of it. I already have.

In one swift movement, I step into the fire, uncaring about what comes up in the smoke.

It Could Have Been Me

by Natasha Davies

The gentle familiar sound of the radio alarm, slowly increasing in volume, brought me round from my sleep. I calmly exhaled as the familiar refrain of John Humphrys introduced the headlines. Another crisis, another business gone bust, another political plot twist, another war some place far away that I had never heard of, until now. I shimmied by shoulders back under the duvet, my cheeks were cold against the icy air of the room, my feet however where toasty in bed socks, tucked under my snoring beagle dog, Thatcher.

An unspoken agreement passed between the two of us as Thatcher opened an eye and lifted his ear ever so slightly. Five more minutes. We agreed and closed our eyes again, listening to the weather forecast. Rain, a cold front coming in from the west, so even more rain, possibly torrential, likely flooding to follow. I moved my chin and mouth under the duvet and breathed in the hot air, the light scent from freshly washed bedding, mixed with Thatcher's earthy smelling paws.

'The dog has to stay off the bed. The dog cannot come up stairs. The dog should sleep in a plastic bed in the kitchen. He barks, he howls, he disturbs my sleep'. That's what you had said, over and over again. Miserable man. You hated my dog and he hated you. Thatcher, such a good judge of character, raising his eyebrows as another fight ensued, taking himself back off upstairs as the doors started slamming. Coming to lay next to me on the bed as I filled the pillow with tears, quietly disappearing when you came upstairs to apologise, or more likely to keep up the momentum.

I tried to think of something else, to get lost in the events unfolding on the news. Thatcher stretched out, yawning, a slight wag of the tail, a come on then, its time to get going, fresh air will do us good.

I hesitated a moment longer, the room was decidedly freezing outside of our bed. I daren't afford the luxury of heating during the day, another jumper, two t shirts and doubling up on socks usually got me through, sometimes a blanket for Thatcher. A brisk walk would help as well, it would make us appreciate being inside later when we returned, I thought to myself as I reached over to stroke Thatcher's long velvet ears. 'Right then Mr. Lets get going'. I felt my way to the bathroom, brushed my teeth and scraped my hair back, pulling on my jeans, busying myself getting ready to face the rain and the biting wind.

Only when I reappeared in the doorway did Thatcher hop off the bed and trundle down the stairs with me. I collected a cup from the sitting room and placed it into the sink. I caught a glimpse of myself reflected back from the kitchen window. I used to look sad, forlorn, but now I just looked tired and thin. I washed up the cup and put it back neatly into the cupboard next to your super hero mug. My fingers brushed the handle slightly, I winced, a memory coming into the light and then fading just as quickly as I shut the door.

Thatcher found his ball and waited patiently next to the stable door at the back of the cottage. I heaved myself into my wellies as I wrapped a scarf twice round my neck, cementing the look with the addition of my wooly bobble hat. It was still gloomy outside, the rain and the relatively early hour elicited a shadowy darkness. Nighttime owl hoots had been replaced by the loud chatter of the crows in the trees at the bottom of the garden. We made our way out across the lawn and through the brambly gap into the woods at the back of the house. While only a small woodland, it was largely unmanaged and left to grow wild so that the coppice was dense, the path overgrown with nettles. Once inside it was darker still. We knew our way around intimately from years of walking here daily, we knew where the turns were on the pathway, we knew to avoid the swollen trip hazards of the tree roots crossing underfoot, we knew where the two little stumps were in the middle of the path, where sycamores had attempted to grow and obscure the entry way entirely, before my Dad had put pay to their plan with raw and determined sawing.

Thatcher was off on thundering paws, ears flapping with the thrill of the chase, a squirrel spotted some distance off, desperately digging up some bounty hard fought at the start of the winter. The rain came down hard against the tree canopy, I was sheltered well in the woods, but once we got out and through to the fields beyond, we were in for a soaking.

I closed my eyes for a second and breathed in the fresh scent of the ancient trees, rain cleansing the ground, readying the dormant seeds for the springtime. Your face flashed before my eyes, an angry image. Your voice hoarse with shouting, unending accusations, a flurry of bile ridden spite. I let out a sob, a guttural moan. I opened my eyes sharply, embarrassed, a consuming sense of having been heard filled my thoughts. I called for Thatcher who came ambling back down the path, his face inquisitorial. I shook my head a 'I'm ok, you go ahead'. The rain dripped down from the hat over my ears. Of course, I wouldn't be heard,

I could sing my heart out here, shout and rage against some oppressive misery, recite The Lady of Shallot at top volume and no one would hear me. Nobody walked these woods, and if by some miracle a rambler decided to attempt to locate this path, they certainly wouldn't be doing it in weather like this.

Thatcher stayed with me for a short while before darting off into the undergrowth after some new quarry. The crows up above us took off noisily, filling the air with a flutter of irritated caws. I couldn't help it, my thoughts returned to you again. Why had it gone so wrong? What could I have done differently?

The counselor had said it wasn't my fault. That it's typical in situations like this, for the woman to blame herself. 'He was a very angry man, he was clearly the one that needed help, he was the one with the problem'. That I was better off without you, that it was the best thing that could happen, no more bruises, no more covering up, no more awkward questions, no more lying to friends and family. 'You are alone now, but you are happier, it will get better, you will start again, you will find someone else' everyone told me, the same mantra repeated until my sadness became all too tedious for them.

I had never been particularly convinced. It had been two years, but I still felt it was a mistake, that you would see sense, that you would come back home to where you belonged. That I could try harder, that I could make things better, that we could work it out. Stupid. Stupid then and still stupid now.

My eyes fully adjusted to the obscure shadowiness, I walked on to the darkest part of the woodland. I could remember walking here as a child, I had felt that I possessed some mystical power, that I was one with the trees, plants and bluebells in the spring. That I could converse with the birds and all of the woodland creatures, that they saw me as their queen, they would alert me to danger, they would swoop in and take me away to a better undiscovered life. I smiled to think of it now, my childish imagination, my safe place against a mundane life, a hostile adulthood to follow.

My parents had retired to the south of France, leaving me the cottage in the vain hope that it would provide me with some stability, it would help me out, give me a purpose, give me a direction. Go to work Tilly, pay the bills, maybe meet someone lovely and have children of your own. Visualise them racing around the garden, building forts, imagining fairy princesses into life.

Happiness, Tilly, it could be yours, this is what we give to you, our only beloved child.

Instead I had met you. You had sought me out, you had cemented your place in my world and then it had begun. A slow decline, the drip, drip of abusive desolation. Nothing less than I deserved. You invaded my home, you claimed my life as your own, you disrupted and alienated.

Thatcher's howl brought me back to the walk. I imagined him, head thrown back, bellowing at some unsuspecting creature, most likely a little muntjac or fast paced rabbit that had managed to get away. 'Thatcher' I called out into the gloominess. I could sense he was somewhere up ahead of me, the path twisted as I carried on. The leaves shone green, weighted down by the unceasing deluge. I reached up to pull my hat further down over my ears, the dampness was gnawing at my bones now, seeping into my creaking spine. Chilling me.

Another few minutes and I would be across the little wrought iron bridge and out into the fields. Thatcher liked a long walk, we usually spent a few hours in the morning trudging through the woodland and then briskly circumventing the ploughed up wheat fields beyond. It was the only exercise I got, I hadn't been near a gym in years. I loved being out with Thatcher, it gave me thinking time, it allowed my mind to heal, to live in the past, but also to make sense of it, to adjust piece by piece. I relished seeing the wildlife I was privileged enough to live alongside, last year I had seen young badgers out near their set very early one morning. Thatcher had whizzed by on the trail of something delicious, completely missing them in the shadows. I had stopped to watch them play, delighted as they grubbed around in the soil hunting out scrumptious beetles and bugs for a snack.

'He did it again'

The voice came from the left of me. I stopped dead on the path.

'Hello?' I called out a question.

Silence.

'Is somebody there?'

Nothing.

I looked all around me. I couldn't make out anyone. I felt foolish, my imagination had run away with me. I called for Thatcher again. I quickened my pace when he didn't materialize. I breathed deeply in through my nose and out through my mouth. 'Take a second' I told myself. 'Just breathe'. Just like the counselor had taught me, a means of quelling a panic attack, a means of dealing with the crippling anxiety you had left me with. I stopped entirely for a second, concentrating on breathing. Sometimes it all got too much, sometimes the memories encircled me, enclosed me into a stone coffin, held me by the neck, choked the oxygen out of my lungs. I looked down at my boots. Two feet, two legs, a body, two arms, head firmly on top of my head, I'm fine, good to go. My ritual thought calming me. The wind blew wildly, shaking the trees and roaring the biting cold up around my face.

'You tried to warn me'.

The voice again, from the right this time. The same voice, a strained, stilted woman's voice.

I was horrifyingly afraid; the rain had frozen me so much that I was shivering. I looked again but saw no one.

'Hello' I called out again. 'Do you need help?' I thought, maybe try to be kind, then whoever it was might pity me, leave me alone, stop trying to scare me. I tasted the metalic tinge of blood in my mouth, once so familiar, I reached up to wipe it away from my lips. Nothing was there.

Silence.

It seemed as if the birds were holding their breath, their calls had ceased. The woodland seemed to be watching me.

'Thatcher' I called out.

I felt claustrophobic, I knew I was being watched.

'I have a dog' I said, 'I don't want him to hurt you, he wont take kindly to you sneaking up on me' I carried on, not sure where to direct my voice, thinking of my floppy eared beagle who would inevitably roll over at the first sign of trouble.

A feeling of someone standing behind me, the heat of another body warming my back all at once took over my senses. I spun round. Nothing.

I heard Thatcher's paws rumbling on the metallic bridge. A sense of relief flooded my blood. I waited for him to appear. He totted around the corner, wagging his tail. 'Where have you been?' I asked, bending down to give him a scratch. He looked up at me, then turned and placed himself next to me, sitting proud and straight at my side. I looked at him curiously, smoothing down his ears with my fingers. 'What are you doing? Are you tired after running around?' I smiled at the top of his head, glad of his familiar company.

Then I heard the clear and distinct footsteps on the bridge. The metal creaked as someone walked over, their movement became noiseless as they crossed and reached the muddy path on my side. I slowly uncurled my body from bending down over Thatcher and waited.

Before I saw, the voice came again, this time from the pathway.

'I should have believed you'. Clear, softer this time, tinged with something.

I looked up, searching the path for the owner of the voice. Thatcher began to wag his tail slowly, keeping his eyes forward, staying guard by my side.

'You were right, you knew, you knew what would happen'. I willed my eyes to adjust, to comprehend to whom the voice belonged, but still there was no one there, no one on the path, but the voice very clearly came from in front of me. Thatcher remained by my side; his tail wagging became more hurried. Then he closed his mouth, looked up at something to my left, his hair smoothed down before my eyes, his head resting to one side as if someone's hand stroked his face.

My realization came quickly, an image flashed to the front of my mind. A recognition, I knew the voice. I knew who this was, yet I still saw no one.

'Cassie?' I spoke out in a whisper.

The warmth of another human reached my side, the closeness of another person entered my senses. A light fragrance detectable, something floral.

'He went too far this time.'

I looked into the space where she should have been, I tried to steady my mind, my eyes searching for her figure. The voice was unmistakably Cassie's voice. Thatcher settled to lie down beside me, I felt a presence rise up, a gaze meet mine. I reached out a hand as if I had lost my sight. I felt nothing. The rain seemed all at once to calm into a light drizzle, the wind dropped, there was a peaceful calm.

'I came to say sorry. I should have listened to you. I shouldn't have spoken so cruelly to you.'

He voice was resigned. I steadied myself, I felt as though I were looking into her eyes, I could picture her now. The last time I had seen her, snarling, fuming at me for going to see her at the café where she worked. She screamed at me that I was making a scene, that I needed to leave them alone, that no matter what had happened in the past, he loved her now, he didn't love me, never had, it was over, I needed to move on, they were happy.

My mouth moved to form an unspoken word.

'You were right, I knew it then, but I didn't listen. He was everything you said he was, only worse.'

I understood then, I knew what she was saying.

'What happened?' I Stammered.

'He hurt me. Like he hurt you. You have to help me.'

I nodded. The years of pain coming back to me, punching me hard in the pit of my stomach. I knew you would hurt her, deep down I knew she would follow the same path I had. That it wasn't me, it was never going to be just me, that it was you. That this is what you did, this is how you were.

'How?' I spoke into the air trying to fix my gaze on what could not possibly be there.

'You have to tell them to look for me at the warehouse, you know where, I'm where he took you."

My vison clouded; an emotional outburst of a memory swept before me. The warehouse where you worked, where I had gone to meet you that day, worried about the previous night's argument. I had brought you lunch, a peace offering. You had smiled to your work mates, asked for a second as they cleared the room. Then you had let the daemon take over you, you had dragged me through the back, held my hair tight in your first, kicked out, screamed at me for embarrassing you in front of your colleagues. You had flung me against a filing cabinet, my ribs cracked, my mouth swirled with blood. You had dragged me down some stairs into a basement cellar. I had blacked out after some time, I don't remember anything else, but when you came to move me, help me up and back out, it was dark. Dark apologies.

I felt as though I were watching the scene play out, and that Cassie was stood beside me, watching it also.

The comprehension of what must have happened to Cassie, what you had done to the woman I had blamed for taking you away hit me hard. Had it not been her, it would have been me. If she hadn't come into your life, mine would have ended.

'Will you help them find me?'

'You are, you're, dead.' I answered, staccato. Frightened of my own words, terrified of my abrupt consciousness.

No answer came. Thatcher stood up and began to wag his tail again. His eyes followed an unseen specter walk back along the path, lightly tread along the bridge. I wanted to follow, but I knew I needed to get back home, I hadn't formulated in my mind how I would go about letting the police know, how I was going to explain how I knew, how I knew where they would find Cassie. How I knew that it was you. You who had done this to her. I was sure I was going to sound like a madwoman, no matter how I said what I needed to say, I might even run the risk of incriminating myself, but I knew I had to help her. I had to make sure she was found and that you were punished this time for what you had done, what you had done to Cassie and to me.

I walked back towards my cottage, my mood lifting, Thatcher at my side, my body and spirit full of gentle determination.

Time and Tide
by Claire Marsh

March 19th 2019

I smooth down the trousers of my formal suit. I want to present myself as professional and competent but, at the end of today's ordeal, how will the public and press view me? Daniel will drive us to the inquest. My hands shake, palms sweaty. The memory of last Christmas hangs heavy as an anchor, dragging me into icy depths. During the journey I'll mentally rehearse my story again. But I'm still undecided – when I testify should I tell the truth? And, if so, would anyone believe me?

*

December 24th 2018

I called at Daniel's cottage to pick up the British Legacy Land Rover. Normally he drove us over to the island, but he'd rung me earlier to say he was ill. I found him holed up on the sofa under a blanket, watching daytime tv, something he always said he despised.

'What's the matter?' I said. 'Is it man flu?'

He managed a grin. 'No, I feel like death warmed up. Have you rung our area director?' 'No need to trouble him. Marion and I can cover today as there won't be many visitors.

Where is your aunt by the way? We'd better make a move.'

'His aunt is here,' Marion sniffed pointedly as she emerged from the kitchen. 'I've left you bread and homemade soup for lunch, Danny dear, and here's a nice cup of hot lemon.'

'You're a treasure,' Daniel hugged her.

'Now dear, I don't want to be catching your nasty germs,' she pushed him away with a coy smile. 'Otherwise who'll cook Christmas dinner for us?'

Before shutting the front door I shouted, 'If we're not back by six send out a search party!'

'I should hope we'd be back well before then. This is the first time British Legacy has made us open up on Christmas Eve,' Marion reverted to her usual grumpy self. It would be a long, long day without Daniel to lighten things between us.

Rounding the bend down to the harbour, then driving onto bright, wet sand I felt exhilarated. The deserted island loomed half a mile ahead – the iconic outline of St Nectan's Abbey a fairy-tale silhouette against the ice blue sky. The golden figure of the saint balanced on the spire glinting in the December sunshine. Jagged rocks surrounded the island and the walls around the tiny harbour over there were sheer. The only access was by the causeway up to two hours either side of high tide, or by boat across Saints Bay.

But there was a chalkboard notice that the ferry wouldn't be operating today. I spotted Tom and wound down my window. He called out from the deck of the 'Isle be back' (his little joke) which bobbed at her moorings. 'There'll be no grockles, I'm stayin' in port.' By that, of course, we knew he meant The Pilgrims' Inn.

'See you in there later for a Christmas drink,' I snorted.

Tom's tufted eyebrows furrowed as he squinted up at the mackerel clouds, 'Mind the weather, could turn nasty later, though it's not forecast.'

'Oh, we'll be back before it breaks,' I said with the complete confidence of the ignorant. A stiff breeze topped the receding waves with white laced foam as I headed for the causeway, driving over the now drying cobbles. Although I tried hard not to jolt us. Marion tutted and clutched her battered handbag.

'It's a much smoother ride when my Daniel's at the wheel.'

I gritted my teeth, 'of course Marion, but do you want to take over?' 'I've never had cause to drive.'

We went over in silence, until I pulled up the steep slope in front of the gift shop.

'I'll start stocktaking. Please give the rooms a Christmas treat, Marion.' She scowled at me. The café was her usual domain. It wasn't my fault we'd been instructed not to open it today. She resented me being appointed her manager, 'A graduate and not a local' I'd overheard her complain to Daniel.

'Yes, Ms Webster,' her lips curled as she emphasised the 'Ms'. 'Just call me Alice,' but I knew she never would.

Only a few hardy souls visited, all wearing hiking boots and expensive cagoules. They were generally self-sufficient once they'd shown their British Legacy membership cards and bought the guidebook. I worked my way through the 'Christmas Fare' which would rapidly lose its charm after the holidays, reducing sale items ready for our return after Boxing Day. Then a book caught my eye; 'Legends of British Legacy Properties'. I'd only worked here for a couple of months and ought to know more of the island's history. I put it aside to browse through during my lunch break.

I already knew the basics – this was a holy island, a place of pilgrimage for centuries and the relics of St Nectan, in the abbey, were reputed to cure any disease. What I didn't know before was that in 1348, when the Black Death raged, a band of pilgrims sought sanctuary on the island on Christmas Eve. However, when they dropped their hoods the black marks of impending death scarred their faces. The Abbott, impervious to their desperate pleas, ordered his men to 'drive them back into the sea, to cleanse them of their sins'. The abbey servants obeyed, stoning the terrified pilgrims with rocks. Injured, they fled to the causeway, which was vanishing under the racing winter tide. Their screams were dreadful, and their leader cursed the Abbott and St Nectan's Isle with his dying breath.

The Abbott went ahead and celebrated Midnight Mass, as if that evening's events were of no consequence. He prematurely gave thanks for their deliverance from the pestilence, while a terrific storm raged around the Isle. But to no avail. The entire population of the island sickened and was ravaged by the end of January. The last surviving monk's written testimony was the only record of the catastrophic events. For many years it remained, like much of England, deserted after the Great Mortality.

'Remarkable isn't it?' I could hear Marion telling the last visitors about our beautiful Tidal Clock. 'It was made in 1786 to help islanders plan their journeys to the mainland safely. Mind, sometimes the clock has played false leading to drownin's.'

The visitors made their excuses and scurried back to the mainland. Her tale had the desired effect – she wanted them gone.

I walked to where the clock stood in the entrance hall. How archaic to trust in something so ancient. We always relied on Daniel's experience of the vagaries of local tides and weather. 'Shouldn't we be going?' Marion moaned. 'I've got so much to do for Christmas dinner; the sprouts won't prepare themselves.'

The walnut case of the Tidal Clock gleamed in the rays of the setting sun, the engravings of The Moon's phases looked impassive on its face. On cue it chimed three times and showed high water at 7pm. Then it hit me; surely the sun couldn't be setting at 3pm. I checked my watch. It read 16:00. Had Marion altered the clock to trick me into leaving earlier? With a jolt I realised if she'd done so she'd have moved the clock forward not back. I felt the first prickle of anxiety. I tried to ring Daniel for advice, but the signal was lost.

'Let's go right now.' I rapidly locked the shop, slipping the keys into my pocket, while Marion turned off the island's generator.

As we hurried to the harbour, I skidded on the stones, dropping the Land Rover keys and my phone into an unreachable, cleft in the rocks. I swore. Marion was livid.

'Look what you've done, now we'll have to walk over fast before it gets dark.'

'Sorry Marion,' and I meant it. 'It should only take us fifteen minutes to cross; it won't get dark for a while yet. I grabbed a torch from the office.'

While Marion as usual was dressed in her sensible flat shoes and stretch 'slacks', my heels and tight skirt soon became a liability as we were on the causeway.

Darkness was falling fast as we reached the half-way point and the biting wind became ferocious. The full Moon rose with an oily halo; in its silver twilight the causeway became a patchwork pathway of iridescent cobbles leading us safely home.

A chain of swinging lights became visible, appearing to come towards us from the shore. I couldn't make sense of them. Even the usually opinionated Marion was stumped. 'Can't surely be fishing boats out tonight?' she sounded puzzled. We heard the growing sound of singing, soon drowned out by a terrific roaring noise. The sea appeared to rear up as the waves hurtled towards us across Saints Bay at the speed of a galloping horse.

I clutched Marion's arm. 'We've got to go back to the island.'

'Well, I'm going to the mainland, come hell or high-water,' Marion shouted. 'I've got Christmas to attend to, even if you haven't.'

A straggle of ragged, cloaked figures approached us carrying crucifixes, chanting, lanterns swaying frantically on poles in the wind. We stopped, trying to take this in.

'Maybe it's a historical re-enactment organised by the Legacy?' Marion said doubtfully. I froze. Surely, I would have been informed if so? The men seemed unaware of us, just focussed on reaching the island. The leader's hood slipped. Marion and I stared into the abyss of human misery in the eyes of this dying man. The hideous sores on his exposed arms and face were livid and smelt of putrefaction. I retched.

Marion screamed, running along the causeway, the waves now lapping at her feet. Arms flailing, she slipped backwards into the water. The lifebelt post was on the far side of the pilgrims. I wanted to help her, but nothing would induce me to pass through their midst. I kicked off my shoes and charged back to the Isle. My lungs burned, feet lacerated then stinging in the salt water. The edge of the causeway vanished under the encroaching tide. Somehow, I reached the shop, unlocked the door and bolted it behind me.

Collapsing behind the counter I sobbed, struggling for each breath. The wind howled trying the windows, rattling them, begging for admission. I remained in darkness apart from the torch. I couldn't contemplate going outside to the generator house. Cut off, no communication, I huddled wet and shivering under one of the Heritage Tartan Throws from the display. Would anyone on the mainland raise the alarm?

Suddenly there was shouting and running footsteps. Perhaps help had come? Or maybe, miraculously, Marion had risen like Poseidon from the heaving sea. I felt momentarily hopeful, then over the wind I could hear screams from the causeway. I'll never know whether they came from Marion or the Plague Pilgrims meeting their recurring fate.

I raided the shop for Legacy mulled wine and I gulped it down, trying to erase the images from my mind. I must have dozed for hours. I woke to distant chanting, surely the Legacy Plainsong CD which played on an endless loop in the abbey during opening hours? Then I remembered the generator was off.

Peering out of the window I saw the impossible; flickering candlelight in the abbey, turning the stained glass into jewelled kaleidoscopes, belying the horror of the night's events. Midnight Mass was being sung.

Throughout the night the chiming of the Tidal Clock woke me hourly and I cursed it, drunkenly blaming it for luring Marion to her death. I realised my encounter with the Plague Pilgrims had saved me from the lethal tide by driving me back to the island. And, had Marion not been so pig-headed about preparing her bloody Christmas dinner, she'd have survived too.

At dawn I woke up to hammering on the door. Daniel and two police officers had crossed over with Tom in his boat. Their faces registered shock at my dishevelled condition. I tried to explain what had happened to Marion, but it was just slurred gibberish.

Marion's body washed up along the coast on Boxing Day, her bloated grey face contorted in agony. Or horror.

*

March 19th 2019

The jury returns a verdict of Accidental Death. I must have sounded deranged when questioned. British Legacy provided legal support, of course, covering their backs over their 'duty of care' towards Marion as their employee – and my perceived deficiencies as her manager in not saving her. The Coroner is compassionate about the terror I'd faced on the causeway with the unexpected storm force wind and Moon-fuelled tidal surge. However, she dismisses my account of the Plague Pilgrims as 'hallucinatory'.

But Daniel believes me, the only one whose opinion I really care about. He heard the fragmented story from me over Christmas and, seeing the traumatised state I was in, somehow knew I was telling the truth.

*

British Legacy has stated that it won't be opening St Nectan's Isle next Christmas Eve.

The Watcher

by Jan Steer

(3ʳᵈ Place)

He was shouting at me now.

"I don't want to think about being in touch with my inner self or about being at one with my thoughts or any of the psychological babble that these head shrinkers throw at me, day after day. I can't take anymore. I've had enough." He stopped talking abruptly then began to breathe heavily, deliberately, as if he needed to think about each inhalation and exhalation before executing the tasks. He stared down at his boots. He was finding just staying alive exhausting. I spoke next. "Not your favourite people then?"

"What?" The surprise registered on his face. "I said not your favourite people."

"Who?"

"The psychologists."

He turned his face towards me, the furrows on his forehead deepening, his eyes looking through mine into my brain as if he was making a gigantic effort to supplant my thoughts with his own.

"They always talk in clichés and that irritates me. Why can't they just say what they mean in plain English? What is wrong with these people?"

He moved his face into his hands, screwing his tightly clenched fists into his eye sockets. He rolled his body around in his seat, rhythmically making monotonous circles under him. It was as if he was suffering the agonies of some internal physical torture, as if a strand of barbed wire was being dragged slowly through his intestines without the possibility of respite, however brief.

"I'm talking about loss, plain and simple, loss, nothing more." Where were his thoughts now? They were so obviously in disarray. There was nothing plain and simple about his reality and there was plenty more that needed to come out of him, for him to explain. His mind had inexplicably deconstructed the delicately configured jigsaw puzzle of his past and jumbled up the separate pieces. Now nothing fitted properly. His world had become complicated; a parody of a surrealist's painting.

I wanted to enter his subconscious mind and heal the wounds that were still raw and suppurating and that had infected his wakeful moments; to ride on his nightmares and lead them, wild-eyed and snorting, out of his blackest skies.

Suddenly he stopped moving and pointed down at his feet. "They've taken my laces you know. My boots slap my feet when I walk and now they hurt my toes."

Quietly I said, "I used to complain about my feet until I met a man with no legs." "Did you?" he asked.

"No. Not really. I think I must have read that somewhere, in a book perhaps and long ago."

He looked me up and down. "You're still in your working clothes. Why is that?" "I'm not sure. There was no time to change into anything else I suppose. Does it matter, is it important?"

His shirt was hanging loose over his trousers and he fingered the hem haphazardly. "No. I suppose not."

"Then, my old friend, why don't you tell me what it is that's destroying you?" I said reassuringly, softly so as not to alarm him further and therefore add to his hideous and problematic mind set. He turned on me quickly and forced his words into my face from behind clenched teeth. "You know what happened," he spat venomously, "you were there."

And now he was shrieking, up on his feet and circling the room with his eyes tight shut, palms pushed to his ears in a futile attempt to hear nothing. "I can't go through it again. I can't speak of it. I don't want to see the pictures anymore. Please …Make them go away!"

I moved to put a comforting arm about his shoulders. I was, however, unable to touch him, not in the physical sense although I tried my hardest to bring him a little peace. I motioned him towards the chair. He understood and dropped into it again. He looked up at me with pleading, red-rimmed, sore eyes and said again, "Make them go away," almost inaudibly.

"Talk to me about it. It will help, I promise you. Have you never heard of the talking cure? The more you do this, the easier it will become you know" I said compassionately.

"Of course, I have! They speak of nothing else in here. The quacks I mean and all the green suited minions who follow them about doing their master's bidding" he added, sneeringly. "But I never talk about it! I told you, I couldn't do that. I just can't separate the words from my pictures, those hideous, hideous pictures."

The situation was becoming more difficult and I wasn't sure whether my presence was helping him or indeed adding to his obvious misery. And, I didn't know how much time I had left with him.

"Then," I said, "why don't you tell me a story?" "What story?" he asked.

"Tell me the story of two men and of what happened to them" I said, "two men who you know very well. Tell it in the third person. You won't be responsible for what they do. You'll just be an observer, a watcher, like me. They can do anything, anything at all and you won't be responsible. It won't be you in the story, just some man you know."

He sat more easily now, though still battling with his thoughts and several more minutes passed before he spoke again. Meanwhile, I said nothing, but stood and watched his struggle from a distant corner.

"OK I'll give it a go" he said all at once, in one exhalation and began. "There was once a sailor", he began, "who had a friend he loved as if he were his own brother." And he cried aloud in anguish as he told his tale of a vicious war at sea; of selflessness and sleeplessness, of camaraderie and of compassion beyond belief. Of grey, confused seas and torn skies, of being cold and lonely - and hungry too. And of his fear, the one constant in his shipboard life. As he spoke, his voice rose and fell like the waves. One moment his words came out soft and controlled, the next screamed maniacally into the fetid air of his room, a room that had almost become his tomb. He talked on telling of the black smudges that moved erratically against the sky which, when picked out and highlighted by the red and yellow streaks of tracer from the guns, grew larger until they revealed their true identities as enemy torpedo bombers.

He had begun to sweat profusely with the effort, the perspiration drawing huge ever- darkening lakes on his shirt. A thick stripe of dark sweat appeared, like a broad painted brush stroke, down his back. He ran his hands over his trousers, continually drying his palms on his thighs.

He bored into me with his sunken eyes, held fast in black sockets and described the chaos as the torpedo struck home. The flash and bang and the column of boiling sea that rose vertically from amidships, of the ominous shudder that ran through the ship from stem to stern as she was momentarily lifted and then flung back again, a dead and useless thing, into the water.

In great pain and shaking with fear, with grief, he talked on with increasing speed, telling of the screams of agony and terror which ran through the ship as she lay on her side, before the stern section broke off and sank without ceremony. Of how one man was catapulted into the waiting sea and of his laborious swim, heavily clothed, towards a floating wooden duck- board and how he had clung on to it for dear life.

His friend arrived at the board almost simultaneously. He had been so horribly wounded that he relied on the man to haul him up onto it and to hold him there as the writhing sea tried vainly to prise each one from their perilous place of safety.

He paused for breath and I noticed then that his face was also floating in an ocean of salty sweat. His nacreous skin glowed like wet putty. He didn't want to continue his journey. His tormented soul was pleading to stay here on this side of the darkness, to stay here where he would be safe. Here he would survive. Further in he may not. He went to his bed and lay down on his back.

"Go on!" I urged, "you must go on!"

"I can't" he whimpered like a little child and placed a forearm across his eyes. "You must," I ordered again. "You must be free of this. You are young, you have a whole lifetime waiting for you outside that door, a life that must be lived in light, not shut away in shadows like these. Tell your story!"

He moved his arm away, placed his fingers gently over his eyes and continued. Slowly and falteringly he began again seeing each picture, in vivid awful detail, behind his tightly shut eyelids. The smoke, the flames, the sinking ship and then the empty oil smeared ocean all around them. Through it all the man clung to his raft and with aching, burning muscles he held his friend in close and screamed words of encouragement to him through lips that were swollen, blackened, cut and bleeding.

How long they were together in that lonely place they had no way of knowing, but the afternoon quickly became a foggy twilight, the air about them punctuated only by occasional shouts and the blowing of whistles by other men, the ones searching for survivors. The lonely hours followed each other into oblivion and still they held on. Unable to speak now, their throats parched by salt and with fingers rendered useless by the intense cold, the two appeared as corpses to the figures behind the lamp in the approaching rescue boat. As its oars dug deeply into the sea, driving the boat ever more cautiously towards them, a British voice shouted to them from high above the wind to, "hold on boys, you'll be all right, the navy's here!" The man raised his head slightly in acknowledgement and tears of relief wetted his cheeks. Their lives were going to be saved and he looked to his friend who, with closed eyes, suddenly relaxed his grip on the board and slowly slid away further into the oil coated sea. Stiff from exposure the man was unable to move or even speak as his friend sank out of sight, feet first, beneath him.

He had rolled onto his side on the bed now and buried his head in the pillow, holding it close to his face, with one hand. Howling like a banshee, with so much expelled grief, he beat at the mattress using his free arm as a flail. "It was my fault. It was all my fault. I should have held on to him, but I couldn't. I just let him go. I couldn't feel anything anymore. There was no more strength left in me!" He sobbed uncontrollably. "Just one more minute, just one and we would have been saved, both of us. Now there is just me. Just me" he whispered in despair. I leaned over him and speaking calmly I said with conviction, "You are not to blame. Death had come long before the body slid away." He stopped crying, looked up at me and opened his eyes wide excited by my revelation. He sat up quickly and swung his legs over the edge of the bed.

"Is that true? Are you sure? You must be sure." His eyes were locked onto mine. He was pleading for his sanity.

"Yes, I'm sure. It was only cramped muscles that were keeping the fingers locked on to the grating. You did your best. You did all you could. It was the wound that ended things, not you. There was nothing that you could have done. The wound was a fatal one. You are not to blame."

Clearly he now believed me, and a modicum of tranquillity had found him at last. With red stained eyes that were both sore and swollen, he stretched himself out on the bed muttering, "Thank God, thank God. I thought I had failed. I thought that it was me…."

The lines began to fall away from his face. He appeared less care worn, less haggard. His eyes were still closed. "Is death terrifying?" he suddenly asked. "No," I said, "people fear death because they think it's something that they're going to experience but that isn't the case. It's as if one moment everything is bright, then the light is switched off and there's nothing; like being asleep without the dreams."

I looked over at him, but he hadn't heard me. I guessed he looked more relaxed now than he had for very many months. He was lying in a deep, refreshing and renewing sleep. I knew that, with my help, he had faced his demons and survived. He could now begin to recover and glue together the building blocks of his yesterdays. Soon he would be able to re-enter the world of the truly alive; a new beginning was awaiting him. His pain would diminish with each re-telling of his tale -

and tell it now he could, but with a very different ending. A painful one, of course, one awash with sorrow, but his wounded mind would gradually heal. The tears would eventually cease.

The blood had congealed into rough lumps along the cuts on the backs of my hands. I held them before me. Through them I could view the room. Although it seemed odd, I hadn't noticed, until now, that my sea-boots were full of water and that my feet were squelching noiselessly in them as I walked about the room. My Duffel coat was also soaked through. The brackish water was dripping on to the floor making small, salty pools underneath me. The left side of my coat was sticky with glutinous blood and as I touched tentatively at the place, my hand sank deep inside, dragging the coat material in after it, and it was then that I remembered. Now I began to appear as something washed out, indistinct, less tangible. I realised that my time here was almost up. I was quickly fading away to nothing. I was being switched off. My plug was being pulled.

I did not know how I came to be here; there were no clues, but it seemed that I'd been given this time to correct a great mistake and save a life. It had fallen to me to dispel my old friend's unjustified torment, restore him to sanity, return him to the world and I was glad of that, so very glad.

Ampersand

by Annabel Hynes

The day had started off with black skies and screaming, so it was fitting that it should manage to include a dead phone battery in the middle of the woods, boots filled with mud, and rabid flies.

Swearing up a storm much fouler than what was rolling up above the treetops, I stomped my way through the underbrush, swiping away branches and insects that seemed intent on settling on every inch of exposed skin. Each time I would slap one away, I'd find another somewhere else, and the flagellating fit would begin again.

"This is so stupid," I shouted, as another branch came perilously close to poking out an eye.

The air was warm as breath, and so thick with humidity that moisture trickled from my hairline and the back of my neck, my impractical sweatshirt and jeans sodden, clinging to my body. My legs were soaked with muck up to the knees, a souvenir from my misjudgement of the depth of a puddle, and my hair swung in rattails matted with sweat, long since torn from its braid. I knew I was a sorry sight even without the new, slender rills of blood that the clawing branches and thorny shrubbery had mapped across my hands and one cheek, the shock of scarlet almost worse than the brief flare of pain upon contact.

I paused at an old fallen tree, the log furry with moss and spotted with brown toadstools. Deciding that I was about as wet as I was going to get that day, I slumped on my rear end with a squelch and rooted in my pocket for my phone. The screen blinked a glowing lightning bolt above a charging port as I jabbed at the power button.

"Oh come on -,"

Suddenly, the screen shuttered completely black. In it, my face stared back at me with almost comical disbelief, and I could hear Claire's disdainful laugh as she jeered at me this morning, last week, all year; I was useless, hopeless. Terrible Terry, can't even get a phone to work, let alone a relationship -

I threw the phone with an ugly scream of frustration, thinking only of how much I wished I had something bigger and more personal to pitch at an unsuspecting tree. I wanted to watch something that mattered explode into shards, a spectacular expression of the helpless fury that was consuming my insides like a disease. I imagined a picture frame, or an old vase, then our TV.

Claire's TV now, I corrected myself viciously.

I felt a light poke at the side of my neck, and looked down to see that yet another fly had made a kamikaze dive towards my collarbone. Surviving the initial assault, it was now crawling up towards my chin. I swatted at it irritably, letting the tiny, sticky corpse fall from my fingers into the bracken. The residue included a single translucent wing, which clung stubbornly to my thumb when I wiped the rest on a nearby boulder.

Close.

I jumped, scrambling back towards the log that still had a patch of crushed moss. The sound had come from nowhere, from everywhere.

Close.

I cast around wildly for the source of the whisper – if I had even heard an actual word – and found only more eerily still verdure surrounding me, weighted with dew and the pressure of the building storm front. I shook my head and hoped that it was just the faintly gnawing hunger that was making me hear things. I would even take the first symptoms of an aneurysm over learning that I was finally losing my remaining marbles.

Close.

The whisper had been bolstered into voice, a monotone that was gaining volume. It was nearer now, and seemed to have a source; an incessant drone that rose from a grassy hollow between two trees. I watched with fascination, then mounting horror as the drone manifested into an undulating swarm of fat black flies, which was twining smoothly between branches as it headed directly for my face.

"Shi-hih-hih-hit!"

I whipped around and took off at a dead sprint, atavistic revulsion sending adrenaline coursing through every blood vessel that had access to my legs. I vaulted clumsily over fallen trees, rocks, clumps of sedge and dead leaves, my only indication of my pursuers the faint tickles of their frontrunners on the back of my neck or in the shell of my ear. My breath rasped harshly up and down my throat, a disgusted yelp escaping when I saw the dark cloud waiting for me by the gorse bushes I had intended to crash through.

CLOSE.

The drone was piercing now, reverberating inside my head and making me retch. I took a hard left in a blind attempt to get some distance, attacking my own face and arms at even the faintest localised sensation. The distinct buzzing followed me for what felt like hours, until I wondered if one of the flies had wriggled its way inside my ear canal. I imagined a black speck burrowing into my brain and coughed out a sob, one errant tear mixing quickly with sweat as I put on another burst of speed.

After a while I came to an unsteady stop, my chest seizing with wracking pain. There was nothing behind me, nothing looming up ahead. Groaning with relief and a soreness that had worked itself into my very bones, I dropped to my haunches, head bowed as I willed my heart rate to calm.

Almost.

"You've got to be joking," I rasped, falling on my backside and drawing my knees up so I could hide my face between them. "Go away! Whatever this is! Christ!"

Almost there.

I chanced a look up towards the new source of the voice, which was no longer buoyed by thousands of miniscule wings beating in harmony. It was a lower register, I thought, like the rasp of a chain-smoker, or –

Almost there now.

The frog was perched on a boulder covered in lichen, its olive-coloured body practically invisible among the hanks of grass until it perked its small head above them to scrutinise my meltdown. Its eyes were black, beady, and unmoving.

"I know you didn't just speak," I said levelly, sanely. "So obviously I'm having some sort of-,"

Please. Almost there now. Almost.

I started. The frog's mouth had opened, all right, and the croak that had come out seemed to have emerged rhythmically from its swollen throat; but its lips hadn't moved. I felt a new type of fear when I realised that on top of that, the words I'd heard were earnest, no longer a coarse monotone.

As though there was a person behind it.

"Almost where?" I asked, cursing myself for indulging what was clearly some sort of psychotic break.

Almost. Please.

The frog's mouth closed, and its vocal sac deflated. It turned around abruptly and hopped off the boulder, keeping to logs and low branches as it headed further into the forest, as though to ensure it remained visible to me. I got up with some difficulty, the muscles in my legs verging on giving up as I set off at a sedate walk behind the frog. It wasn't travelling very fast, nor actively assailing me, but I was vigilant for an army of its friends appearing in my periphery. I slapped my neck out of habit, and looked at my hand. Nothing.

"Will you tell me who you are?" I said desperately, as I followed the frog down the side of a shallow gully at a skid. "Why did you send flies after me? Are you going to kill me? Oh God. Am I dead right now?"

If frogs could glare, this one would have. I stopped talking and focused on hiking through underbrush that looked like it hadn't been touched by human hands in decades – if ever. The air was still and stifling, the lack of a breeze all the more apparent as I panted, feeling as though I was breathing underwater with middling success. The sky above was low, bruised blue with tinges of yellow. It looked sickly, I thought, and despite the fact that I was dripping wet already, I wished for the inevitable downpour sooner rather than later.

The frog had vanished into a family of ferns, and I stumbled through the thickly sprouting leaves in a panic, afraid to lose the only guide I had in this place. When I arrived on the other side the little creature was nowhere to be found.

"Oh for the love of -,"

Better now. Much faster.

I yelped, jerking back from the fox that had slipped between a pair of saplings and bounded to my side.

"I have had just about enough of this shit," I gasped, clutching my abdomen. "Are you the – the same thing? The frog? And the –,"

Yes. Easy talk with big. Hard talk with small.

The fox had orange fur and bright, intelligent brown eyes. There was, however, an eerie disparity between the natural curiosity of the animal and the voice – more articulate, pitched higher with a softer timbre than heard previously – which emanated from its gaping, unmoving jaw.

My nose wrinkled automatically in disgust, and I drew back. "So you are a person. One person." I squinted at the fox. "Are you a person?"

Not now. Not long time. The fox darted in the direction the frog had been so stridently hopping, then circled back to my feet. Need help. Help find?

"Help you find what?"

Help find me.

The fox started loping through the grass as I digested this cryptic description with more than a little doubt. Despite this, not even a minute had passed before I began to jog after it, hacking like the survivor of a burning building.

We had been running for some time – at a desperately slow pace, but still – when I recognised my surroundings as more than just a steady stream of green and brown in various shapes and sizes. There was an increasing amount of tree stumps here, old and smoothed by years of fungal growth and nestling animals. They kept growing in volume as we pressed on, until they were more numerous than the living trees, their bases far thicker than the few birch and ash sentries that had obviously been too young to bother culling. The ground was clearer, too, mostly carpeted with snapped twigs and the mulch of dead leaves, and the lack of foliage had revealed the sky in all its slate-grey glory. An ingrained memory itched, and I scratched it obligingly.

"We're near the quarry, aren't we?" I exhaled sharply. "We've come miles, all the way to the damn Summerby quarry. I remember my dad talking about it, this old clay mine -,"

No.

The fox, which had been cantering along with its head held high as though on alert, paused and scurried back a few feet to match my sluggish steps. It didn't elaborate.

Big drop. Far. Now close.

The voice was faint and breathy, not nearly as threatening as the susurration of flies bearing down on me had been, but I shuddered instinctively anyway. The guileless canine face of the fox twitched, the human noise spilling out only after a gravid pause.

Hurry now. The little beast made a guttural growl, the barest hint of foam rising at its leathery lip.

"Why are you bringing me there? It's been shut down for years now. It's a death trap." I wrapped my arms around myself, wondering what time it was, if Claire was worried.

Probably she had blocked my number already, like she swore she would, in between the thrown plates and bottles. "You said you wanted me to help find you. What does that mean?"

Big drop. Down far. Now close.

"Yeah, I got that. You still haven't -,"

The fox ran ahead, dipping in and out of sight between logs and stumps until it was just a red blur in the foreground. I rolled my eyes and tramped on, hoping that whatever strain of pneumonia was currently invading my body held off its throes for at least another few hours.

I passed more of the standing trees, stepping over desiccated boughs until I found a clearing that was mostly grass, and when I looked up I found a chasm.

The quarry was perhaps six hundred feet deep, but with mezzanine-like protrusions of rock jutting out in shelves all the way down to the bottom. It resembled a giant stairway, the stone dull and gritty with gravel even after decades of being abandoned, though I could see a few tufts of brittle grass between the broken slabs of stone closest. Above the quarry, there was a thin stripe of white on the horizon, a valance of ragged black drifting with reaching fingers towards the distant earth. It was dark as dusk now, though I knew I'd slammed Claire's front door around mid-morning.

"What am I doing here," I mumbled, and turned around, almost running smack into a fully grown adult male deer.

Not so fast.

"Jesus!" I skittered back, remembering the ledge behind me in enough time to catch myself and freeze in place. The deer was tilting its head curiously, its mouth open, tongue lolling out and back in as though tasting the air.

Storm is coming. The voice, I could hear properly now, was pitched high, and rasping slightly, as though vocalised in the midst of a bad flu.

"Yeah, I know," I retorted. I was cold, sweating, exhausted, and finally somewhere recognisable that offered a landmark in the vicinity of my town. The anger that had sustained my rush into the woods to escape Claire, that had borne me through assaults from thorns and nettles and flies and insanity – it had dissipated, like smoke. I had nothing left, only a void where it used to be.

The deer snorted, saliva dribbling into the white fur of its thick neck. Will you help me?

"Help you with what?" I said irritably. "You've been dragging me all this way for hours, telling me nothing. Who are you? Why are you hiding in the mouths of all these frigging Bambi characters?"

Sorry about that. The deer scraped at the ground with its hoof, as though embarrassed. It dipped its head slightly. Cannot speak much, before. Hard to talk. Even now.

"You're doing just fine at the minute," I said, deciding to ignore the starkly ridiculous fact that I was conversing with a woodland animal. A part of me wanted to run, screaming. The rest of me pointed out how much energy doing that would require, which shut that simpering part of me up.

Thank you. I will try. My name is Blythe Summerby. The deer tossed its head again, like it was dislodging an insect. My name. It's mine. Many years pass – I have not heard my name.

I stared. "Blythe Summerby. As in 1950s gumshoe drama Blythe Summerby? The heiress that went missing?"

Heiress. Yes. I have a fortune. The deer's eyes were unblinking, liquid and black. Everybody likes my fortune. Men like my fortune. A great deal.

"The missing Summerby daughter is like – our town's most famous legend," I said, firmly refusing to examine my reality at that moment. I knew I wasn't dreaming - it was too bizarre, though that wasn't very reassuring either.

I am missing, the deer continued, because I am at the bottom of that hole. I have been screaming for so long and no-one can hear me. They talk too loud, to each other, to cameras. Everyone is too far away.

"So you send flies to attack them?" I couldn't really keep the disgruntled tone from bleeding into the question.

Only you, said the deer. Most run away. But you were in pain. Easier to talk to someone else in pain.

"I had a bad break-up is all," I muttered. "I'm totally fine. Just. Perfectly fine." I shifted my weight uncomfortably.

I can see someone who is alone like I am alone, and they can see me too. I think the hurting can stop.

The deer made a keening sound and backed up as though frightened, causing me to swerve away in another bout of caution. It scraped at the ground again, then straightened up once more.

I am so close. Almost gone. Please help. I am down there.

"How – why -,"

There is quartz underneath. No clay. The deer whined. Quartz for stones to put on gold rings.

It bucked its head, the velvet antlers swishing through the air like brandished weapons.

I did not want a gold ring and so the man who wanted me pushed me and I fell a hundred miles and the snow filled the hole and Father stopped digging and the man stopped digging and most of me returned to soil but not all -

The voice did not seem to be coming from the mouth of the deer anymore, but from inside my own head, my blood going cold when I felt my jaw start to creak open.

Take me home. I cannot be strong anymore.

I coughed as her voice died away, my throat rubbed raw and aching. I could hear her now as well as feel her, a thin, reedy wail that was drowned out by the sudden belch of thunder that roared overhead, a following curtain of rain sweeping across the quarry in a silver arc, drenching me instantly. A gentle wind picked up, cool on my skin.

"Okay," I whispered hoarsely. "I can do it. It's okay."

The rain fell in sheets that pooled quickly as I began to navigate my way down the quarry. There was a thin path carved into the side of the cliff face that excavators must have constructed years ago for regular use; it was slightly overgrown with weeds and brush, but I chose my steps carefully and kept one hand against the rock on my left side, the cuts on my palm reopening and leaving small smears of blood that were quickly washed away by the storm. I descended for almost an hour, absent-minded and giddy from the clear air, my weakened limbs barely hindering my progress.

It soon became difficult to see a few yards ahead of my feet through the rain, let alone across the ravine, but something soft at the back of my mind pulled me in one direction. The cries had been reduced now to a sombre humming that increased the further I trekked across the floor of the quarry, stumbling over the detritus of dead animals and live ones, fallen trees and leaves and hail, brocade, worn threadbare by the ages –

"Got you," I said breathlessly, pulling away branches torn from their boles by wind, scooping up handfuls of mud, dirt, and stone ground so fine it was almost dust. A brown skull grinned emptily at me between ribs and bones long enough to be from a pair of legs, likely nosed about by something hungry after a bad winter. I stripped off my sweatshirt, which was thin enough to be useless in the still torrential rain, and gathered the bones into the makeshift sack. Some of the smaller ones I slipped into the pockets of my jeans, fingers and toes and teeth collected like loose candies. The humming continued, but now at the timbre of a lackadaisical gardener, not the whine of an inmate in solitary confinement.

"Let's go home," I tried to say, but all that came out was a wet cough, my chest twinging with every inhale. Let's go now, passed through my mind with some urgency, and I strode through the rain back towards the path I had struggled down, counting every heartbeat where it pulsed against the chipped skull. I cradled it like an infant, letting it face the lightening sky until it was cleaned of grime, the toothy smile senseless, euphoric.

***

"Thank you," said Jason Summerby, shaking my hand for far too long. "My grandfather is in tears, he can't believe his sister is finally back. I really wish you could come over and meet him -,"

"Maybe some day," I said generously, ignoring the loud vibration of my new phone from somewhere to my right. "I'm just glad I got her back to you."

"You told the papers you thought her fiancé did it," said Jason, fidgeting with the hem of his jacket. "He's been dead for years now. Why do you -,"

"Seems obvious to me," I said lightly. "Not that it matters. The main thing is that she got back to the people who loved her, you know?"

"Right." Jason gave me a genuine smile. "Anyway. Please don't be a stranger. Granddad won't stop talking about his sister and the hero…"

I grimaced. "Well, I mean, I'm not supposed to be going outside for a while, according to my doctor. So -,"

"Oh! My God, of course," he said, and offered me everything from a cup of tea at his grandparents' nursing home to an appointment with his family's photo albums whenever I wanted it. I managed to shoo him from my parents' front porch after several minutes of this, waiting until his car had left the driveway before leaning against the door and sighing.

I picked up the phone slowly and unlocked it, scrolling through messages from concerned aunts and enquiring friends from college, interested in my five minutes of fame in the local news. Claire's name was nowhere to be found. I looked at her name in my contacts list, her number installed there from memory.

Something smooth was in my hand, being turned over and over again in my idle fingers. I glanced down in surprise and saw that I had taken up the index finger-bone of Blythe, left behind in my back pocket when the nurses had returned my ruined clothes to me. It was ivory-coloured and persistently cool, no matter how long I held it in my grip. I deleted Claire's number, still rolling the bone like a magician with a coin. If I focused, I could hear content humming in the back of my head, a melodic aria soft as water.

No Rest for Merry Gentlemen

by Josephine Rummage

(Children's Runner-Up)

1853, Christmas Eve

John Remperton rubbed the grubby coins between his fingers nervously, lest he should drop them down a gutter. Anxious to buy it, after saving up for weeks, he entered the shop.

"Yes, that bear, with the green ribbon. Thank you, dear man. Goodnight, and Merry Christmas." The doorbell jangled as he stepped out of Old Cedar's Toys. Ten shillings he spent on this soft animal. Some bitter misers would yell "Outrage! Downright scandal!", but his response to these condemning words would be alike any other father who had just freely given away his savings for the benefit of a small child; a gracious smile and hearty laugh, much to the dislike of the unworthy opponents.

He fixed the bow straight on the toy, grinning.

Green, to match his eyes.

The cold seeped through his skin and clung to his bones like frost, as usual for a late December evening. Shivering slightly, he drew breath. A rising chorus of "God Rest Ye Merry Gentlemen", his all-time favourite carol, filled his heart with warmth, whilst the taunting smell of hot gingerbread cookies wafted up his stinging nostrils.

The fluffy layer of snow muffled his footsteps as he strode out onto the path, cradling the bear like an helpless infant. Courtesy of a recent snowfall, which had coated every surface imaginable with the thick, icy substance, the roads glowed white in the darkness. A carriage clattered past him, leaving long tracks, winding off into the distance. He then proceeded to cross over to the jolly festivities of the town square.

A steam carousel stood to his left, with overjoyed children clinging to the backs of gaily painted horses, bobbing up and down. How simple entertainment is, yet it brings so much happiness, he thought, smiling to himself a little as he surveyed the youngsters. Crowded refreshment stalls circling the square made his mouth water, for the tantalising aroma of roasted chestnuts, boiled sweets, warm mulled wine and sugarplums is enough to make a man of strongest resolve weaken.

The largest attraction to this man though, was the towering pine right at the centre of all the merriment. A huge choir huddled together, enrobed in white, beneath the richly decorated tree. A small throng of persons stood before the warblers, singing along in all tones of voice. He accompanied them, for a minute or two. The enticing proceedings of the square had him sidetracked, for he had meant to go straight home.

He stood there, mind absent, admiring with twinkling eyes the sparkling tree. The same feeling that overcomes every soul at Christmas settled upon him; the tranquility and magic of a knowing that somewhere in the vast world families are cared for tenderly and peace brims up in hearts young and old alike. Visions of innocent lambs hanging their stockings upon the hook, eyes shining at the thought of Saint Nick sweeping past the moon, dashed through his head. Christmas can even be greatly surprising when the most prickly of hedgehogs unfurl and openly share any ounce of compassion they can muster.

Candles held by the misty-eyed carollers let off a warm glow. Gazing musingly at the flickering lights, for an acute moment he believed they would not for a second falter. But each and every flame must expire in time, mattering not how healthy or carefree it may seem in the beginning. Snapping back to reality, he turned abruptly on his heel, determined to arrive home in time for supper.

He took the usual route, through the alleys. It was dark where the snow could not reach.

He walked briskly, his long ebony coat sweeping just above his ankles. As he ventured further into the gloom, a feeling of uneasiness settled in his gut.

His eyes began to dart this way and that in a foreboding manner, his nerves tingling at the slight hiss of a cat.

He began to tell himself that he'd been reading far too much Dickens, that his mind was merely playing wicked tricks upon his eyes. But the shadow flitting in and out of his vision through the disconcerting fog seemed to be more than a figment of the most vivid imagination. Any sense of warmth and security he'd felt had now diminished.

He wandered through alley after alley, unnerving and baleful, twisting like a never-ending labyrinth beneath the pale moonlight.

And he was very much alone.

Spindly shadows stretched themselves tight as catgut across the cobbles, like the hand of death greeting many an unfortunate soul who stumbles into his wake on a cold winter's eve. As night set in, the air dampened around him, his spirits swiftly following suit. The choir was just a small noise in the distance now, like the creak of a floorboard when one is half at rest.

But the melody of the carol still rang out merry in his head:

O, tidings of comfort and joy. Comfort and joy!

O, tidings of comfort and joy.

Concluding that he was, indeed, alone, he decided to sing. His voice fell out hoarse and echoing, breaking open a path before him in the thickening silence. But this jolly chirp seemed only to attract more alarming presences.

His footsteps rebounded off the walls as faster and faster his head did spin.

He was running now, running faster and faster, the blackness reeling around him. Then he heard the song.

A sinister ditty that caused his pulse to quicken and palms to sweat. The voice was old and croaky, cruel and impish:

"God rest ye merry gentlemen, let nothing you dismay..."

A swish of cloth startled him, chest rising and falling much too quickly. Utter darkness.

Yet the haunting tune continued to carry along the stone.

"No rest for merry gentlemen, when fear comes out to play…"

Across the path ahead a figure flickered past. And this time John knew it was not his mind. Sweat dripping from his brow in late December, he stood statue-still until his heart slowed. Eventually he found the courage to take a step forward.

And another. And another.

Constantly reverberating around him, the quaint tap of his boots knocked at his ears, like the undesirable thoughts nagging to enter the vast chambers of his mind. Breath rattled through his teeth and misted on the air as an inexplicable dread crept slyly up his neck and into his cheeks.

'Twas then that he spied a single, flickering light, looming from the dark like a wisp. Naturally he expected his primitive instincts to kick in at any second.

But they didn't.

He was transfixed.

As the mystical glow drew nearer, he saw that the source was nothing but a lantern dangling from a staff. A rather anti-climactic discovery, might you unknowing readers bleat, but alas, you have not yet seen, as has our John, what was holding the staff.

Revealed to him by the faltering firelight, a most repulsive form he saw. Toward him hobbled a crippling, raddled hunchback, supported solely by a hand-willowed staff measuring taller than himself. From every single crevice sagged abnormally pallid flesh as a tattered brown cape hung off his limp shoulders. Each and every hair was grizzled and streaked with white. Out of a face so shrivelled in its proportions that the owner could only just make out the newcomer peered two sharp, taunting eyes as black as the sky above, striking an unfathomable mixture of deep uncertainty and hesitation into John's heart.

He did not trust this man. The cunning countenance he held so eloquently unnerved him greatly. For a moment he stood stock-still, dumb for words.

The decrepit man was first to speak. John instantly recognised the voice.

"Beest not alarmed, mine knave, I meant not to setteth thee affright." The wicked eyes glittered maliciously, and John knew much better than to trust his word.

Silently he waited.

The old man blinked, evidently realising that amiable charms would have no effect. "What a lovely bear thou has't, such a marvellous ribbon," he admired, a dilapidated hand reaching down to the toy that John was clutching. The father noticed and hastily snatched it away.

A bit too hastily.

The cripple fixed him with a cold glare, flames dancing devilishly in his eye. "Peradventure I could giveth thee a token of fine craftsmanship for thy bear," he suggested softly, eyeing it with greed.

John firmly shook his head. "Not a chance in heaven, dear man, for it is for my son upon Christmas morn." With that, he concealed it in the folds of his coat, defiantly looking down his nose at the man.

The elder stared back up his own nose with a pitiful air. This only fuelled John's temper. "Stand down, man!" he bellowed, forcing him aside. "Step back hither, sir! Or thou shalt payeth the price!" croaked the old man, shaking his staff in anger.

"I have no interest in your offer!" called John stonily, not turning back.

The man continued to bellow after him, dancing around his staff like a spritely elf. "Leaveth tonight a candle burning bright, beest it undisturbed 'til the morning light!" Idle threats, thought John.

Idle threats.

*

He stroked the forehead of his beloved son as he snored gently. He smiled.

"Timothy, how I adore you," he whispered, hanging the boy's stocking, which held the bear, from the hook. Then he stepped backwards and observed the scene with satisfaction. Nothing lit the room but for a fire in the grate. John caught sight of a misplaced candle in the corner of his eye. The stranger's words floated back into his head, and suddenly his form went tight. It wouldn't hurt, he thought. So he proceeded to light it and place it upon the mantel. He then retired to the cherry- coloured armchair by the fire.

He dozed in the velvet easy chair for quite some time, humming to himself, fire crackling away. Admiring the small pine upon the dresser, lovingly adorned with popcorn garlands and red bows, he pictured his wife.

Her smile haunted him in the best way imaginable. He shut his eyes, chuckling a bit to himself.

The flowers she would every Saturday purchase would sit upon the sill.

The memory was so strong, so vivid that he could almost smell the spice of geraniums. He exhaled.

Inhaled.

Something caught in his throat.

*

The waves lash against the rocks and break through the crags. Gulls wail overhead, circling above the choppy waters.

The crash of the sea is deafening, the cool salty mist soaking through my clothing.

Breathing in nothing but salt, I choke her name.

"Lenore!"

Through the confusion I see her.

Her back turned to me, arms spread wide. Wet dress swaying in the wind.

The sea grows stronger. Angrier.

Something stabs at my heart like a dagger.

No.

I step towards her. I stumble.

The jagged terrain cuts into my ribs, knocking the air clean out of me. Vision slurred, I croak her name once more.

"Lenore!"

I watch as a colossal wave rises high in the air. And descends over the rock.

Lenore.

*

He awoke with a start.

Tears clung to his lashes, and some had already fallen loose. His hands jittered uncontrollably.

Clenching his fists to suppress this tremor, he took a painful second to remember where he was. The clock on the mantel ticked away, the sound drawn out excruciatingly.

He exhaled.

He was at home. Not by the coast. He wondered how long he had slept. And his query was answered as if by clockwork, for the horologe on the mantelpiece chimed half past one.

He wearily shifted in his seat, looking around.

Through the black room swept an eerie chill, the cause of his shivers. Wide open was the shutter, clattering against the wall. Bone-cold and bleary-eyed, he rose.

Ever so cautiously making his way to the window, he stopped. The moonlight shone in, uncaring and bright.

A certain twinkle in its face forewarned him of something. Something.

Lip trembling slightly, he drew the shutter closed. Wringing his hands, he staggered toward his seat. He had not the strength to venture to his bedroom tonight.

As he sat, his soul swam with menacing thoughts.

A terrible feeling of knowing possessed him. Suddenly, he realised what had unnerved him so. Slowly, his head turned to view the bedsheets.

The still form of a child's body was a mere lump under the covers. And a simple sound was missing.

A sound most take for granted. Breathing.

He let out an almighty sob as it dawned on him what had occurred. But it was already much too late. It was done.

He turned his head to look at the candle on the mantel. It had flickered out.

His son was long dead.

He collapsed, knees weak and shaking. His heart tore in half as he sobbed, loud and distinct. Then he heard the song.

A sinister ditty that had caused his pulse to quicken and palms to sweat.

The voice was old and croaky, cruel and impish:

"God rest ye merry gentlemen, let nothing you dismay…"

He howled only louder.

"No rest for merry gentlemen, when fear comes out to play…"

"WHAT HAVE YOU DONE?" he screamed in despair, pounding the floor with his fist.

"Once more a life is taken on this merry Christmas Day. O, tidings of comfort and joy, comfort and joy!
O, tidings of comfort and joy."

Bound for Eternity

by Grace Dodridge

With more than a hint of trepidation, I took the keys. The young man at the estate agency was barely out of school, with flapping fingers and mannerisms that magnified my own discomfiture. Wiping his hand on his trousers, which did nothing to erase the dampness, he jumped up and thrust it forwards, grasping mine in a vigorous shake. There was a keenness in his face, eyes bright behind the metal-rimmed specs and hair combed sleekly with a side parting. His patterned, woollen tank top, paired with beige corduroy slacks, completed a picture reminiscent of an earlier age.

"Well, good luck, Mr Moore. If you have any questions, you know where we are."

I paused for a moment to consider. Would the question be too intrusive? Surely it was only natural. "I was wondering why the owner decided to pass the property on in this way. It's rather unusual."

His fingers began clicking and he licked his lips. "Well, Mr Carruthers never did things in a customary way." He gave a nervous giggle. "With no relatives, he was keen to find a book lover to continue the shop." He paused as if more was to follow, then stopped himself. "Well, as I said, I wish you the best of luck."

I was beginning to believe I would need luck. Stepping out onto the Square, thoughts raced through my mind. Was this a mistake, to move the family here on a whim? The thought had seemed absurd when I sent off my bid to the silent auction, drawn in by its strange prize: a second-hand bookshop, fully stocked. With my meagre offer, the possibility I could win seemed so remote that I'd discarded it from my mind.

By the time I opened the envelope relaying my success, my heart was divided. I'd been harbouring second thoughts. Martha had embraced the whole idea without hesitation, considering it a late Christmas present. "A new start for a new year, and what better place for a wannabe writer to be inspired? It's fate, it's meant to be," she'd grinned.

So here I was, keys in hand. No turning back. The deeds stipulated that the premises must remain a bookshop. It might be every author's dream and my own pipe dream, but it was a massive undertaking, and one that risked burying me alive, considering my lack of retail experience. I supposed I could always sell it on if things didn't work out.

The town was quaint, with an olde worlde charm plucked straight from a Dickens novel, though it lacked a certain bustle of excitement and purpose. It was one of those places people visited for Christmas stocking fillers rather than made their permanent home, and in the mid-January mist the town cast a gloom that I couldn't imagine ever lifting.

Buttoning my coat, I ducked my head against the squall which was blowing in from the sea, and forged forwards to the other end of the High Street where Ghost House Walk was tucked between a tearoom and a junk shop. It was so narrow I would have missed the entrance if it hadn't been for the signpost. The alley held a remarkable stillness and it was a relief to be sheltered from the wind. The overhanging buildings blocked out what little natural light there was that day and I had to watch my step on the cobbles. No signs of life were evident in the houses to either side.

Then I heard a creak and looked up to see the dangling sign in front of me, jerking as if buffeted by a billowing, solitary gust. BILLY'S BOOKSTORE. I smiled. Martha had laughed at the fortuity in the name. It was meant to be. She'd dismissed my proposal to upgrade it to 'William's

Books'. "It sells used books, Will," she'd said. "The name's perfect. If you modernise it, it'll lose the quaint ring." She was right, as always.

I stepped back to get a proper look at the building. It looked solid despite its age. The red brick, half-beamed, Tudor-revival style was attractive, its three storeys beckoning. It was difficult to see through the window with its uneven surfaces distorting and reflecting images. I pressed my face against one of the leaded panes, hands cupped around as I peered through.

Whack! A thump above my head made me jump round. "Aaargh!" A lacerating blow to my scalp made me lurch and I braced an arm protectively in front. "What on earth …?" Then I edged back against the wall, heart pounding, scanning the alleyway. It was empty. It took a few moments to ease my gasps while I leant on the wall for support, extending one hand to the crown of my head. There was a dribble of blood but nothing to be concerned about.

Then I spotted it on the ground. A pigeon was twitching, struggling in his final breaths, its chest heaving; then its eyes glazed as its legs extended out in front and all movement ceased. I saw the imprint it had left on the glass and felt a weird desire to laugh.

"Oh dear, the poor love." I started at the voice in my ear. A woman with crinkled-paper features was watching me. "Didn't have any idea, did he?" Her stare was intent and her face too close, her breath stale but warm in an invasive way. Before I could respond, she'd nestled the bird in her hands and was walking away with it. I felt a grimace rise to my lips as she glanced back, her expression ambiguous, her long, brown skirt dragging on the cobbles.

"No, I suppose not," I said to myself as she disappeared, shaking off the strangeness of the encounter. Then I began fumbling in my pocket to extract the keys. As I pushed open the door, it triggered a jangle reminiscent of old shops. It seemed to resonate for a prolonged moment before leaving a deathly silence. I envisaged an elderly man shuffling out from a back room, but there was nothing except the whistle of a draught that followed me in and fluttered the bunting draped across a bookcase.

Even when I closed the door, a rising tide of cold continued ebbing past my feet. I flicked the light switch. Everything stilled and dim lighting ceated an amber haze, casting faded shadows across the floor. I placed higher-wattage light bulbs at the top of a mental list for the ironmonger's I'd spotted on the High Street.

Although narrow, the shop extended a long way back, with a polished wooden floor a warm shade of honey that drew me in. Bookcases unfolded before me with row upon row of packed shelves, the assorted hues of the books' spines bringing the room to life. I ran my fingers across the nearest shelf, palpating the solid oak, inhaling the familiar aroma of patinaed wood. Yes, Martha would approve.

My foot caught on the loose threads of the rug beneath my feet, jolting me forwards. That was a trip hazard and would need removing. I smoothed it out for the time being and made my way down the aisle, running my hands along the ends of the bookcases as I peered into the alcoves either side. The shop was embracing me, beckoning me forwards. I could imagine us settled here, Martha writing and the girls snug in armchairs in an alcove, poring over novels. The excitement was seeping through my veins and I felt compelled to call Martha.

As I tapped my pockets for my phone, a whiff passed by. It smelt different back here, a strong herby aroma penetrating the air. It wasn't unpleasant but powerful, like an apothecary's dispensary, a scent to ward off ills. I could imagine the shelves crammed with potion bottles and jars of dried leaves, scales with brass weights on the counter, a queue forming out the door in years long past.

Then a trickling sound from the back room drew my attention. Pipes had a habit of gurgling in these older places, a reminder that original plumbing remained untouched. I'd spent my childhood in a Victorian house with its assortment of creaks and groans so was accustomed to the sounds; but something in this noise was sending a creeping up my back. Nearing the rear of the shop, the chill in the air descended suddenly, turning into an icy heaviness that crushed my chest. A constriction in my throat forced out a wheezy cough. As I gasped, a misty vortex grabbed me in its centre, disorientating me; I whirled around, seeking an escape from the centripetal force, my arms grasping for something to hold onto. But there was nothing there. It lingered an age compressing, stubborn, refusing to turn me loose, suspending me in a nebulous haze. Then, just as suddenly, it released me from its grip, leaving the spinning in my ears to fuel my nausea.

Fumbling in my pocket, I found my inhaler and dragged a couple of puffs to steady my breaths before sinking into an old armchair, dribbles of sweat dampening the collar of my jacket. The chill passed and gradually my nerves settled. It was fine, merely a panic attack passing through like a whirlwind, leaving me feeling a trifle foolish.

Then I became aware of the trickle again. It was gentle at first. Then it escalated into a gushing lasting a few seconds before coming to an abrupt halt with a juddering of the pipes. I listened intently, peeling off the tongue velcroed to the roof of my mouth, itching for a drink. Then the cycle recurred. Trickle, gush, judder … trickle, gush, judder. Then it crescendoed, louder and louder … the cycle speeding up until it was just gush and judder … gush and judder …

There must be a tap in the back room, turning on and off … on and off. I clutched at the table to steady myself.

"Hello …" I croaked.

Silence closed in all around.

I cleared my throat and forced a steady voice. "Hello … anyone there?"

The silence pounded in my head, the absence of creaks and groans and gushing all the more ominous. But I held my breath steady, ignoring the racing in my chest as I eased my feet forwards. Was it my imagination or was the air chillier near the door? I reached out before snatching back my hand, scalded by the icy doorknob. Stop being ridiculous, I chided myself, kneading my hands in a frenzied attempt to erase my unease.

Then I gripped the knob firmly and tore the door open. It released an arctic blast that gushed past as I clung to the doorframe. A muffled sound of giggling children hung in the air, jostling either side of me. There was hair blowing across my face as their lingering presence enveloped me. For a moment, time felt suspended.

Then, as it swept away, I was left in eerie silence once again. I fumbled for the light switch then peered into the back kitchen. It was empty, but the back door was ajar, letting in a breeze that billowed the curtains into ghostly lifeforms. I hurried to slam it closed, shutting out the …

Then the whimpering began, first as a gentle child's snivel, building up to a soulful wail that drifted down the stairs in waves, ebbing and flowing over and over, their intensity searing with each cycle. The sound penetrated all my senses; even when I clasped my hands over my ears it seemed to seep through my skin, the sonar pulses echoing through my body.

I was drawn involuntarily up the stairs, gripping the banister for support as the steps creaked one by one. My own sounds halted the wailing until all I could hear was my shallow breathing coming out in quivers. I wanted to stop but my legs marched to a silent rhythm. The further I ascended, the sharper the chill, until my breaths misted up in clouds before me.

There were voices in the room to the right, soft murmurings in answer to a child's bleating cry. I stopped outside the doorway, fearing what lay inside, but the sounds went silent. My legs were threatening to buckle and I steadied myself against the wall, forcing the contents of my stomach back down as I did so.

Then I pushed myself forwards, fighting the urge to squeeze my eyes tight. In the corner of the room a woman slouched against the wall, her eyes, ringed in dark shadows, penetrating mine. They were soulless, unmoving, but bore into me with a vengeance. Then I noticed a movement on her lap; it was slight; a groan was followed by a child's pitiful cough, breaths fast, body barely responsive. More disconcerting, another child's lifeless body lay beside her like a discarded rag.

She looked up at me, through me, mouthing words I couldn't hear, before she too began coughing, a scary chesty heave that choked the words away. Still her relentless stare would not release me. She beckoned, holding her child up towards me, a child so deathly grey beneath the blankets. I edged forwards, unwilling yet unable to resist, stretching my arms before me. Then, as she reached skeletal hands forwards, her eyes melted into hollow sockets, her breath gusting in my face, the apothecary's poultice enveloping me in a suffocating embrace. My cry was stifled, stuck in my throat. It turned bitterly cold as I felt the children's bodies sweep past again, their laughter in my ears, this time with a sinister, echoing ring. Stockinged feet ran down the stairs.

I spun round in a vertiginous frenzy, frantically searching, for what I didn't know. The room was empty, the corner bare apart from a dirty blanket with its reek of herbal potions. But the apparitions remained firmly fixed in my mind. My gasps caught in my chest, making me collapse to my knees. I wanted to cry out, but there was no sound. Nothing.

Until a solitary creak rose behind. I turned. The door across the landing inched open slowly, too slowly. I was consumed in a trance, moving my legs forwards, my steps resonating.

My eyes were cast downwards as I eased open the door, somehow instinctively knowing what I would find. I didn't see where the light came from to illuminate the solitary figure. The polish on his boots reflected my fearful expression, his revolver fallen to the floor beside him, the battalion of his soldier's uniform unknown to me. I didn't need to look any further and tried to back away, but the invisible pull was lifting my face, forcing me to see. It was putrefying, what was left of his head, maggots crawling to create an intrusive reek that assaulted my senses. My hand reached my mouth and I gagged, my eyes shutting out the horror before me as I fumbled my way back onto the landing. Feeling a heaviness in my head, I clutched at the wall for support. The cold passed through me again and I turned away, crouching, willing it to pass.

It must have been barely moments before the air returned to normal. I knew that it, whatever it was, had gone. I seemed to half-float, half-stumble down the stairs, my eyes struggling to focus. Then, as I reached the warmth of the shop floor, there was a jangle. The front bell was ringing, persistent.

"Who's there? Who is it?" My voice was sharp, and I could hardly recognise it as my own. I didn't expect a reply and braced myself.

"Hello, luv', I've come from the tea shop. Thought you'd like this." A young woman was carrying a laden tray. There was something familiar in her look, the wild, disconcerting eyes. "We met earlier … that poor pigeon …"

"Oh, yes …" Was that really her? She looked younger now, or maybe it was the light. Her face was innocent, lacked the watchful creases that age and unwelcome knowledge etched on one's features. She placed the tray on the counter and turned back towards me. I flinched, horrified at the transformation. The girlish smile had morphed into an older woman's vacant countenance, the gaze remaining equally intent but terrifying. I wasn't certain how long I held my breath before she released hers with its stale smell. What happened to that sweet-faced girl?

Then she turned to leave, scuffing her feet across the rug. When she reached the centre, she tapped her foot, her head shaking. "Let them rest in peace." With that, she glided off silently through the front door into darkness.

I hurried to the door and pulled it open. The moon was casting a faint glow, the alley succumbing to nightfall. There was no sign of the woman, old or young.

Bending to my knees, I rolled back the rug, watching dust clouds rise into a puff of smoke intent on choking me. As I rose to my feet, coughing, the door jangled. An unintentional cry escaped my lips.

"Sorry, Mr Moore, didn't mean to scare you. Just thought I'd check everything's all right. I was passing on my way home." The estate agent stood on the threshold hovering, his earlier smile more hesitant and his nerves as frayed as before, if not more.

It took all my restraint to stop myself from throwing my arms around him. I knew he'd feel the shiver passing through me and question my sanity. Even I questioned my sanity. "Come in, come in please." I knew it sounded pleading.

He was reluctant, his gaze resting on the space where the rug had been, fixated and silent, and suddenly the silence felt overwhelming. "Ah, I see you've discovered it."

"The cellar? Yes, the young lady … old lady … whoever she was from the teashop, she mentioned it."

A fearful look passed over his face as he searched my eyes. He was trembling, backing away, his arm reaching for the door.

But I beat him to it, holding it closed. "No, you can't leave without telling me what's happening."

"Please …" He tried to grab the door handle from me, but I was by far the stronger and wrestled him away before turning the key and slipping it into my pocket.

"You owe me an explanation. What is this place?" I gestured around the shop as he slumped onto the stool behind the counter.

There followed a deathly silence before he spoke, his voice tenuous and eyes still not meeting mine.

"This bookshop was opened by the Thomas family over one hundred years ago. William Thomas was a writer and playwright who was showing great talent, so people said. But when the Great War started, he was drafted along with everyone else, leaving behind his wife Clemmie and two young girls. He wrote daily, fought for them, survived for them. Then tragedy struck. On his return, he discovered that Clemmie and his daughters had succumbed to the Spanish flu only days before …"

"So he shot himself …" I finished the tale for him, startling him into looking up, and he could see it in my eyes, what I'd witnessed. Then I had to ask, a hysterical laughter building up within. "What happened to the man who owned this shop before me? He died young too, didn't he?"

He watched me closely as his voice adopted a hesitant whisper. "Mr Carruthers … he isn't dead. He is a resident at Oakmead."

"Oakmead?" I'd passed it on my way into town. "An old people's home?"

"No, not exactly. Oakmead is a psychiatric hospital. Mr Carruthers' mental health declined after he suffered his own tragedy." He spoke deliberately but what was unsaid spoke louder.

"What happened?" I was pretty certain I didn't want to know but at the same time I needed to.

"Before Mr Thomas blasted his face away all those years ago, he made a couple of stipulations: firstly, that his bookshop should forever remain a bookshop; secondly, he also requested that his family tomb should remain undisturbed in the cellar. And for many years, generations of owners have honoured the request.

"Mr Carruthers, however, was keen to redevelop the property and had plans drawn up. No one saw the accident, but screams were heard. Mr Carruthers, who had been in the cellar with the architect, rushed up to find his children lying motionless at the bottom of the stairs. Onlookers swear that there was an eerie sound of laughing children upstairs following the event. Since then, poor Mr Carruthers has never recovered, swearing that the Thomas family want to exact revenge." He went silent for a moment, then his voice was barely audible. "Of course, we all know that can't be true."

There was an icy stillness around us as he spoke, and I knew that he could feel it too but neither of us would acknowledge it. I don't know how long we sat there terrified to move, but eventually he helped me to unroll the rug, the tremor through his body as clear as mine, and together we placed it back over the cellar hatch.

An icicle slithered down my spine as I locked up and handed him the keys. We made our way back to the main street, where the gale had turned to a gentle breeze. It lifted away the heaviness that had descended around us, and we parted company.

On Monday, I would send him instructions to sell the property.

Top of the Stairs

by Kate Fleet

By the time we stepped into the gabled, red brick porch of number sixty, it was snowing hard. I was glad Jack had parked around the corner and we'd walked the last two hundred yards or so to the front door, instead of having to manoeuvre our heavy old Ford Anglia up and down the narrow, slippery driveway. The particulars described the house as a cottage but as we approached, it seemed to me too large for that, with dramatic-looking chimneys and a roof that sloped down over the windows like a distinguished old brow. Set back from the road at the top of the hill which led into the town, its long-residing current owner was Mrs Tellabow: a dignified woman of advancing years who, I knew, had once owned a successful antique shop in the town centre. She had a no-nonsense air about her as she invited us over the threshold.

'Mind the rug, don't trip,' she said as she motioned us to come further into the hallway. 'I'm fond of the place, but—' she broke off. 'Well, it's all just getting too much for me now.' She finished with a gesture towards the rather steep stairs, once-sparkling rings on her wedding finger dully catching the light. After a brief pause she gathered her cardigan about her and retired to the warmth of the sitting room, with its leaded-light windows and glowing fireplace, leaving us to explore at our leisure.

The front door was made of thick, dark wood, with only a small window of pale yellow glass to let through that afternoon's weak, wintry light, and thus the hallway was rendered rather dim. The deep moss-green carpet on the stairs was worn right through in places, the light fittings were of a fashion long past and it was uncomfortably chilly on the landing, but these were minor drawbacks and, as we thought, easily fixed — and there were three good- sized bedrooms, a nook that would make for a cosy playroom, two real fireplaces and even a pantry.

I stood at the window at the top of the stairs, looking out over the large back garden with its mature trees and long beds slumbering under a blanket of snow, and a sudden shiver skipped down my back. I turned to find only that Jack had appeared behind me.

'Someone walk over your grave?' he grinned. I laughed at my own nerviness and gave him a playful slap. He slipped his arms around my waist and then, surveying the scene together, we agreed to waste no time in offering the asking price and headed back down the stairs, hands moving along the thick, ageing paint of the banister rail, to tell Mrs Tellabow our intention. Jack explained that we needed more space now that we had welcomed Elizabeth into the world too.

'A baby girl,' she repeated, then, 'How old?'

'Twelve weeks,' I replied, feeling a smile appear upon my lips.

'Precious treasure. A blessing,' she said quietly, before ushering us out of the door.

* * *

The next morning was bright and crisp, and Charlie was up early, desperate to play in the snow in our tiny garden. In his little hand-me-down blue and red snow suit, he built quite a snowman, while I nursed Elizabeth under the warmth of an heirloom Welsh wool cloak.

Meanwhile, Jack paced with eager anticipation, waiting for nine o'clock when he could telephone the estate agents' offices in Brannock town centre, and tell his long-time friend and associate, Bernard, that we wanted to buy the house. As we'd left the day before, the snow had stopped falling but it had iced the roof like a fairytale gingerbread cottage, and further charm was added by a lantern that glowed in the porch. I smiled at the memory and then at Charlie and his slightly tipsy-looking snowman.

Jack went to make the call. When he came back outside, his face was solemn. He said he was going out to the bakers to get the Saturday rolls and disappeared through the side gate. I could tell something was afoot and my heart sank; we'd already lost out on one place we'd liked because the owner claimed to have had a visitation from her dead husband, telling her not to sell. It was a shame he hadn't visited a bit sooner, before all her belongings were packed up in boxes and our hearts had become set on the spacious 1920's house that was in walking distance from the town centre and local school.

Jack returned some time later without the rolls — a giveaway that forced him to confess what he had not wanted to tell me earlier: shortly after our visit the day before, Mrs Tellabow's nephew had tried to get her to put the house up for auction, using sealed bids.

Jack had heard the news from Bernard that morning, and had wasted no time in visiting the old lady himself, to see if he could talk her round.

There had been no need.

As Mrs Tellabow opened the front door, Jack told me, he'd opened his mouth to begin the speech he'd been preparing but she quieted him with a raise of her hand.

'Mr Stevens, I know what you are going to say — and I can assure you the house is not going to auction. I want you to have it. You've a wife and children to think of and —a family . . . your little girl . . . well, I think perhaps it's just what's needed.'

Of course at the time nothing in what she'd said struck us as strange; we simply felt a great surge of relief at her decision which confirmed to us how much we truly wanted the place and to make it our home.

* * *

Within a few weeks we'd moved, Mrs Tellabow having quickly found desirable accommodation in the town centre, with a favoured window that overlooked the moss- scattered churchyard of St Michael's.

Our life fell into a routine, as it tends to do when you have a young family. The playroom served us well in the few remaining weeks of that winter and when spring came, Charlie was in his element in the garden, never tiring of putting his rabbit in the trailer of his plastic tractor no matter how many times it hopped out, while in summer little Beth crawled on a blanket in the shade of the plum trees.

Yes, in the day time they were contented children but at night, it must be said that they were not good sleepers, and our evenings were not the relaxed affairs they might have been. Our usually placid Charlie would not go off unless his night light was switched on with — and he was adamant on this — his door closed firmly. If either of these items were forgotten he would yell uncharacteristically until we came rushing back from halfway down the stairs to make things right for him. When Elizabeth reached toddlerhood, she took to walking along the landing from her room to ours and slipping into our bed, complaining of bad dreams and 'seeing shapes'. She would climb in, press her freezing little feet against me then fidget in her sleep for the rest of the night.

The most unsettling times, though, were when we would hear crying which stopped when we reached the top of the stairs, investigation revealing both of our children to be asleep in their beds. Whoever had responded to the false alarm would, in some bafflement, tiptoe back downstairs to the warmth of the sitting room. Jack found these instances to be a nuisance, a disturbance; for me, they were disturbing. Because it started to happen in the day time too, when he was out at work, Charlie was at play school and I was alone in the house with Elizabeth. Or, as I'd come to realise, not alone. With the sound of crying from somewhere upstairs, and soft footsteps on the landing, I was cloaked in a sense of melancholy. If I ventured up there, the air was cold and seemed charged with a despair that was almost tangible; the very walls seeming suffused with a mournful longing.

* * *

'Someone's calling out,' remarked my mother from her spot at the end of the sofa one Boxing Day night. My parents had come to us for Christmas and we were gathered together in the sitting room, ready to watch an episode of Poirot on television. It had been a busy couple of days, of course, with two excited children, and sherries had been duly poured once they were settled upstairs. Jack turned the volume down on the set and we all listened.

There was the indistinct but unmistakeable sound of a child's voice. 'Yes, you're right,' I said, 'I'll go.'

'No, no, you stay there,' said my ever-energetic mother, getting up from the sofa and heading for the door. 'And I think I'll have another sherry please, Jack,' she added, handing him her glass as she passed. Two minutes later she was back downstairs with a strange look on her face.

'Everything alright, Kathleen?' Jack asked, although it was quite clear that it wasn't.

She accepted the refilled glass and took quite a swig.

'Well . . . the children, they're fine. Both fast asleep, in fact. Cried themselves back to slumberland, I suppose, whichever one it was. I mean, I couldn't tell which one it was, could you? Usually I can.' She peered at him, clearly turning something over in her mind. 'Anyway, I'll tell you what, Jack, it's freezing up there. Is the heating not on?'

'Yes, of course it is,' he replied, sounding affronted. 'The house is warm as toast.' 'Yes, down here, it is,' she returned, with a slight shiver. 'You go upstairs and feel for yourself.'

I'd already confided to her about the noises that came in the day time too; about the disquiet I felt. We exchanged glances.

'Well?' my mother asked directly when Jack returned.

'Bit of a nip, I've adjusted the thermostat,' he replied, then sunk down into his chair and turned the television up. He didn't say much for the rest of the evening.

* * *

I decided I had to broach the subject directly with Jack. I felt on edge whenever I was in the house alone; tense whenever I heard crying. Was it Charlie or Elizabeth — or another little one?

'Do you know much about who has lived here before?' I asked him one evening as we sat together, he idly watching television, me working away on knitting the sleeve of a cardigan.

'Not really; why do you ask?' I paused.

'I'm not sure I want to say,' I replied. 'Why on earth not?'

'I think you'll think I'm ridiculous,' I said, and then spotted an error I'd made ten rows back. Irritated, I started to unravel the wool.

'Why are you bringing it up then, if you're not going to explain?' he asked, impatience creeping into his voice.

'Because I'm almost certain you won't believe me.' I put my knitting down. 'But I have felt something upstairs, Jack. You know full well it gets strangely cold on the landing sometimes. And those noises we hear at night, I hear them in the day too, when you're at work. Never anyone there but there's . . . there's a presence. My mother felt it too.' Jack said nothing so I continued, 'I think whoever it is — was — felt deep despair or pain or . . . I don't know but whatever the reason, they're still here — and I don't know how to make them leave.'

'You're tired Maggie,' he sighed. 'You just need a few decent nights' sleep. Maybe you should try a hot chocolate with rum in it before you go up tonight? I'll have one too.'

My face felt suddenly hot. I stared at him, but his eyes remained on the television drama, where a row was blowing up. 'Unbelievable,' I thought as I returned to my pattern, feeling isolated and angry.

Over the weeks that followed nothing changed, no matter how many warm, rum- sprinkled drinks I swallowed.

* * *

Sad news reached us, albeit not entirely unexpected: Mrs Tellabow had passed. The funeral was to be held at St Michael's with the wake to follow at her nephew's house on Greenville Road. We decided not to attend the latter, knowing as we did how furious James Tellabow had been with his aunt for selling her house to us, quite likely hoping for a nice extra bit of inheritance. It seemed not quite the occasion to make his acquaintance.

The Revd David Nichols led the service and afterwards moved among the mourners in the churchyard, ably dispensing comfort. I knew he had lived across the road from our house for many years, and when he inevitably made his way over to where we stood, Jack introduced us both properly for the first time. The conversation turned, naturally, to Mrs Tellabow and Jack observed that the house was quite large for her to have lived alone in for such a time, especially with a considerable piece of garden to manage.

'We were a bit surprised she hadn't downsized sooner,' he added. Nichols looked at him, considering.

'Well,' he said slowly, 'I suppose all that had happened there made it rather difficult for her to leave. As well as to stay.'

'You mean with her husband?' I asked, thinking that memories of him and their life together might have held her there.

'Well yes,' he said, 'that.' He made a signal to his wife that he would come over shortly then added, 'And all they had lost.'

'What do you mean?' Jack asked. 'I thought they had a successful local business and retired in comfort?'

'Oh yes, on that front. But money isn't everything, so I'm told, and it certainly can't provide comfort to a troubled soul. Only God can do that.'

With that, Nichols' services were called upon again and he excused himself with a handshake and a promise he would come over to see us some time. The few remaining mourners started to drift out of the churchyard and we headed for home.

* * *

Spring arrived once more and, for me, a need for change: I went on a mission to decorate. We'd done the bedrooms as soon as we could after moving but, with finances tight, we couldn't complete everything we wanted to right away.

The part of the house that really needed attention now was the hallway and landing.

The old, worn green carpet that ran all the way through was one of the less desirable features that remained from the Mrs Tellabow era, and perhaps had been there even before her. One morning I ripped it up in a cloud of dust, with a strength and determination I'd forgotten I was capable of. We all spent the next few weeks wearing slippers and avoiding the exposed carpet tacks on the stairs.

I decided to take all the wood back to its natural appearance, as it would have been when the house was built. I threw myself into it wholeheartedly, using a heated stripping tool to work away at the thick, ugly paint which coated the hand-crafted banisters, skirting boards and door frames. I spent hours at a time on the stairs, scraping away, the smell of burning lingering in my nostrils when I went to bed at night. I refused all offers of help from Jack. It was my project, and I felt driven to see it through.

One Sunday I found out why. I was working on the newel post by the top step and as I scraped, a distinct scar in the wood was revealed. I stopped for a moment. Jack was out in the garden, picking stones out of the terrible soil that blighted the rose bed. I called to him from the window at the top of the stairs. The children were playing in the sandpit with Lucy, the neighbours' daughter who was home from university. By the time he reached me I'd scraped back enough paint to reveal another mark — oblong, neat, making a pair.

'Look,' I said, as he reached the top step. 'And here.' I pointed to the opposite side, to the frame around Charlie's bedroom door: a hole the right size to accommodate a small latch was clearly visible. Until now it had always seemed an insignificant notch in the wood.

'You realise what they're from, don't you?' I asked him. Jack considered for a moment.

'Well, they look like hinge marks to me. From an old-fashioned child's stair gate.' 'Yes, exactly. I knew there was something up here. No wonder Charlie won't sleep with that door open.'

And as I ran my fingers over the wood again we both heard, for the first time at such close quarters, the cry of a child that was not ours. Soft and other-worldly at first then becoming louder, until the anguished sound swirled all around us, filling our ears. The sense of despair was thick and cloaking, and we stood with our backs pressed to the wall, skin turned to gooseflesh, unable to do anything for the poor little soul we could not see but felt, standing close by, somehow trapped and calling out in pain and unhappiness; a child who could never now be comforted. As those words from Mrs Tellabow rang in my head, I recalled her gesture towards the top of the stairs and the air turned icy cold.

It's all just getting too much for me now.

When quiet eventually fell, the air felt still as though the house was holding its breath and I don't remember how long we sat on the bare floorboards before we both picked up the tools at our feet and, together, silently finished scraping the very last of the paint away, before packing everything up and going back out into the garden. We felt like sleepwalkers ourselves, and the late afternoon sun took a long time to make us feel warm again.

* * *

I could never have dreamed how I would make that discovery. That night we had a long, hushed conversation about what to do, including asking the vicar for help. Later, in the hours between the dead of night and dawn, we were roused by a familiar tread on the landing. We waited for the door to open and for Elizabeth's shadowy little figure to enter the room, but it didn't; the steps passed by.

'You see to her,' I said, before turning over.

'She responds better to you when she's sleepy,' Jack replied truthfully.

I sighed with resignation, threw the covers back and made my way to the door. As I opened it, the top step creaked, then there was the sound of little footsteps slowly making their way down the bare wooden stairs. As I stepped onto the landing I hit a pocket of freezing cold air and I knew then there was no point going down to look for our daughter; in the end that's not why I went.

The chill had stolen down the stairs and along the hallway; I had the sense of icy fingers brushing my ankles as I passed but I can't be sure to this day if I really heard a child's laugh, so faint and ethereal was the sound. I looked in each of the still, hushed rooms on the ground floor of the house and when, shivering, I went back upstairs and peeped into her room, sure enough, Elizabeth was in her bed, slumbering soundly with the soft toy dog she'd had since she was a day old, tucked under her arm.

Early next morning Jack and I found that a step with a particularly prominent carpet tack was stained with blood, and the dried red-black marks continued on down into the hall, becoming fainter then disappearing just before reaching the front door. We stood in silence for a while. A biting draught blew sharply through the old, uninsulated wood and glass.

'It's about time I got that seen to, isn't it?' Jack said, putting his arm around my shoulders.

* * *

In the afternoon, we walked over to the churchyard to lay some flowers on the grave which was now dedicated to the memory of both Mrs Tellabow and her husband. I had just placed some lysianthus and a hard-won rose by their headstone when something caught my eye. I hadn't noticed it during the funeral as it was obscured from view by mourners, but now my heart lurched as saw the tiny grave next to theirs, and read the name upon the headstone.

Evie Tellabow, 1925-1928

I spoke quietly to Jack, who was standing with his hands in his pockets, gazing up at the steeple. He knelt down to read the inscription then held my hand and gently squeezed it. Without another word, he reached over to take the rose from Mary and Walter's grave and placed it on their little daughter's then, in thoughtful silence, we walked back to a house that was peaceful in a way it had not been for the past fifty years.

A Phantom Fair

by Estrella Burgess

(Children's Highly Commended)

Wind blew through the open window setting a chill in the nursery, a child shivered; indisposed from Influenza.

Trying to warm itself, it got out of bed and went and sat by the fire.

Turning to look toward the window, it gazed, mesmerised by the snow, unknowing to the darkness; only perceiving the light.
A shooting star, or maybe Santa…
A child's mind works in ingenuous ways.

Footsteps.
A woman entered the nursery, tall and slender, silhouetted against the grey wall.

"Come my child, 'Tis cold outside, you will never recover if you do not sleep" she cooed.

The woman shut the open window and drew the curtains closed.
"Saint Nick has begun his travels my dear" She then knelt down and scooped up the child,

placing it in its bed lovingly "Now goodnight my darling, may you be well soon and Merry Christmas".

The lady had one thing right, 'twas cold outside, but no Saint Nicholas rode the sky's this Christmas.

No, a much more sinister phantom skulks along the cobbles tonight, unapparent to a child's eye, perceivable to perhaps the more worn at heart.

*

An elderly man of about seventy-five lay in his bed; engrossed in a particularly gripping novel. No fir tree adorned his living space, no mistletoe hung above the fire; the place was bare.

For Charles Bearn the season of winter had always been a time of mourning, of despair.

No light beheld his abode but a single oil lamp, running on the dregs of its fuel.

Eyelids slowly closing, he felt himself sliding into the peace of slumber,
But only to be awoken by a gust of icy wind, snow drifted through the window,

And then a light.
A pale, ghostly light.

As it drew nearer he could make out a figure, a phantom, a luminous apparition.

*

I was at a fair.
It was held on the lake every winter, I recognised the tall figure beside me, my mother.
I looked to my left; my father.

We were on our way to the Ferris wheel; it had always been a tradition to get sugar plums and have a go on it.

The soft tinkling music of the carousel filled the background, giving me the shivers that child gets a Christmas.

I held my mother's brown-suede gloved hand, warm around mine, yet I felt uneasy.

The screaming started off distant, then the sound drew nearer; a cacophony.

I looked over to see my father being dragged along by the crowd, "look after Charlie!" He cried as he disappeared.
I turn back to look at my mother, she looks terrified.

"Charlie" she says, trying to sound calm, although I can hear the panic in her voice.
"You're going to have a go on the Ferris wheel"

And at that she leads me to the wheel, picks me
up and places me in the carriage lovingly,
"You're going to be fine honey" she says ruffling
my hair, putting her navy-blue coat around me
and shoving my cap onto my head.

I giggle and look up at her
She smiles; stroking my cheek, and for that
moment, all the screaming and yells were dulled,
all the firelight, all the horror.
Blocked out by a mothers loving gaze.

I stare up into those warm, soft brown, tear filled
eyes; to mirror mine.
Then as quickly as the feeling had come, it's
over.

She pulls the lever to start the ride and stands
there waving as I rise higher and higher.

Watching her wave at me, I can't help but to sob.
There's no one else up here to see me anyway.
I reach the top and come to a halt, I see my
mother run into the distance, a boy of eight;
alone.

I would normally have said the view was
beautiful,
Because it usually was.
But no.
Not this time.

The deserted fairground, shattered ice, the
smouldering wrecks that were once beautiful
rides, adored by children and adults alike.
I watched long enough to see a luminescent,
cyan figure drag a woman with brown-suede
gloves beneath the ice.

As the phantom dragged the woman under I saw
by the light of the creature Itself; the silhouettes
of dozens of bodies against the underside of the
ice,
A mass grave.

I shiver, pulling my mothers coat around me, I
drift off into sleep.

*

I now recognise this being, the same spirit that
took my parents, the same phantom that eternally
ruined the festive season for me.
"What do you seek here?" I ask.

Silence.

hand and beckons, I hesitate.
It expects me to follow.
A great force tugs at me, as if it's reeling me in,
the world seems to spin before me.
My only focus is on the creature as I pull my
navy hand-me-down coat around my shoulders.

I feel myself sway, a dazzling, gloved hand is all
I see before I hit the ground.

*

I awaken, the view is beautiful, I'm atop a Ferris
wheel.
The fairground below is bustling,
The singing of a choir, a festive setting.

Families having fun, children screaming; In
delight.

I would normally have resented this scene of
splendour, the happy faces, the sweet aroma.
But there a sort of ataraxia about me, that which
I had only felt Sixty-three years ago…

The presence of a mother.

I turn to my right, there sitting before me is the
phantom.
This familiar sensation can't be coincidence.
It turns to look at me; warm eyes.

Blue like the rest of the creature.

But warm.

Mother

I now know, they are at peace, my parents, all
those people, at peace.

I also know, this phantom is and will always be;
an omen of death,

A reminder for the weary at heart of the
deceased, their deaths, seem less sad now.

Almost…warm; like her eyes.

I sigh.
Death must take us all one day, at some point or
another…

After a long life, such as mine
Or maybe a sudden one, a sadder one, like a
smudged painting, a record finished too soon.

I gaze into her eyes, she reaches up and strokes
my cheek, her gentle touch…

A revenant of my parent...

I feel my hands grow Icy, the darkness closes in,
I lean back and enjoy my last minutes of life.

Oh Mother, I can't wait to see you again.

*

And at that moment a spectral light,
an unwelcoming phantasm, enters a child's
nursery,
ever so softly making its way over to the child's
bed.

The little hand on the pillow grows cold as the
air outside and limp.
The face; not unlike its mothers, pales as the
Infant breathes its last breathes.
Never to unveil the wonders, the delights, hidden
away in the stocking at its feet.
The remedy at its bedside, unneeded.

Taken too soon.

Death must take us all in the end.

Papa Salvatore

by Philip Gibson

(2nd Place)

Simon lay in bed, eyes wide open, catching the shapes of shadows projected against the wall as car headlights slid past his window. A fertile imagination is the enemy of sleep and eight-year-old Simon's imagination was prolific. He saw repeatedly, the outlines of claws hanging menacingly on outstretched arms and monstrous heads with dripping fangs hovering high above his bedside table, only to disappear as the vehicles passed by. His curtains did their best to shut out the invasion, but modern halogen bulbs are like lasers and hyper-efficient in projecting the silhouettes that spark fear into an eight-year old's psyche.

Simon ducked down underneath his duvet being careful not to snag the bandages on his left arm. His right hand emerged and delved under the bed grasping what appeared to be an anglepoise lamp in miniature. The lamp was a stocking filler gift from last Christmas, and Simon valued its discrete size and effectiveness. Take off the plastic coin shaped base and the arm could be slotted into the top of a book creating a handy yet ingenious micro-reading light. In addition, the battery seemed to have magic properties; having never faltered at its task to generate light.

Apparently, according to his mum, this form of undercover reading was bad for his eyes. Simon's logic had worked out that this might be a case of a parent making stuff up to achieve whatever aim they intended to achieve. Clearly the light was good for his eyes as without it he couldn't make them work. In the face of this kind of manipulation, Simon had decided that subterfuge was a reasonable response. If his mum didn't know then all was OK. However, there was a problem. He hadn't factored in his dad.

"Is that a monster under there?" came a deep, yet soft, growling voice. Simon started with a gasp and then giggled in recognition. Simon's giggle was like a high-pressure squirt of contagious joy.

"I'm coming to get you!" the low volume disembodied snarl continued. Simon threw back his quilt, a massive grin stretching from one side of his face to the other.

"Dad!" he half whispered; half shouted. "You're back! Tell me a story."

"It's late. You should be asleep." His father responded switching on the bedside light and switching off the mini anglepoise torch.

"I tried but I'm not sleepy. Tell me a ghost story. I like them." Simon ordered enthusiastically.

"I can't do that – it'll scare you to death and then what'll mum say. What's that you're reading under the duvet anyway?" His dad picks up the book Simon had under the bed cover. "Mmm, sounds educational - 'The ghost in my toilet' – I bet that's a best seller!"

"It's great, dad. Tell me a story. One of your made-up ones. I promise I'll go to sleep."

"Oh alright. You cuddle down though while I think." Simon's father sat on the side of Simon's bed and put on an exaggerated 'I'm thinking deeply' type face.

"Perhaps you can help me," he said, "what do you think this story should be about?"

"Make it about a boy and his dad going on an adventure."

"I can do that…. Ok are you ready?" Simon nodded in response. #

"One strange day, when the clouds were low in the sky and the hills and mountains felt rather squashed, there was a little boy called Symeon who wanted to go on an adventure." Simon smiled at the mention of this name and the similarity to his own.

"Symeon wanted to escape the gloomy valley where he lived. The people in this valley had to walk doubled over so their heads didn't disappear into the murky fog-like haze and spent all their time looking at their feet mumbling to themselves about the length of their toenails and their corns and bunions.

Symeon dreamed of looking up. He didn't care about toenails or corny onions. He hated the mist, the fog and the heavy boulder shaped, grey clouds pressing down on his world. Symeon thought the clouds carried misery and despair, while he dreamt of laughter and light. Symeon would simply have run away and escaped the valley, but there was a problem. The high sides of the valley and the low earth skimming clouds met to form a barricade that circled the entire area. To leave, Symeon would have to brave going through the forbidding mass of cloudy vapour. No-one had ever done this before, or at least, no-one he knew about.

However, on a particularly gloomy Thursday, Symeon could bear it no more and he climbed the valley side to the point where clouds met land. A constant drizzle seeped into the earth making the grassy slopes spongy and difficult to walk on, causing Symeon to stumble awkwardly as he reached the top. Symeon stared into the grey trying to catch a glimpse of what lay beyond. The foggy mass churned and boiled as if alive. Every so often he thought he saw an ominous shape, the fangs of a werewolf or perhaps the claws of an ogre but, whatever it was, it soon disappeared to merge into the background.

He approached the cloud gingerly, pressing his hand and arm into the morass of swirling particles. Something or someone bit down on the arm and Symeon withdrew it quickly with a shout of pain. His arm was a mass of red blisters and it hurt. Symeon sat down despondently cradling his arm and blowing gently on it to ease the sharp burning pain he felt.

He was shocked to hear a voice coming from behind his head. 'Symeon, to get to the other side you must protect yourself.' Symeon spun, still holding his arm and saw a light at the edge of the cloud that hadn't been there before. In the light was a figure. It was man shaped but indistinct and it was wearing what appeared to be a long silver-grey cloak."

"Is this the boy's dad?" asked Simon sitting up.

"It might be", replied his father. "Now lie back down and I'll continue."

Symeon stood up and walked closer to the figure. The light surrounding the figure seemed to pulse more brightly, while the cloak wafted gently in response to the roiling grey clouds.

'Who are you, what are you?' Symeon asked.

The figure replied, 'I am a light-spirit. I am known as Papa Salvatore. I look out for people and help them escape the fume- clouds. The fume-clouds are dangerous. And, there are demons around.'

'I think I've seen the demons.' said Symeon, 'and I think I've experienced the danger too!' He raised his arm tentatively to show off his wound. 'What should I do?'

The light spirit was silent for a few moments then stated. 'You know the clouds are dangerous and you've seen the demons, so what do you think you should do?'

Symeon thought about this for a few moments and then replied, 'I suppose I need to find a way to hide from the demons and to cover my body completely to protect it against the clouds.'

'Well done.' replied Papa Salvatore. 'You have found the way. Take my cloak.' Saying that he unclipped the garment and, with a flourish, spun it towards Symeon.

Symeon picked up the coat, which rather swamped him, and walked towards the light spirit. 'Which way should I go?' he asked.

'Follow the light', replied the spirit.

Symeon covered himself with the cloak and followed Papa Salvatore into the cloud, ignoring the savage snarls of the skulking demons. It took some time and it wasn't easy, because he kept having to cover his head if the cloud swirled too closely or a demon lurched into view and the ground was uneven and often marshy, but eventually he reached the end of the cloud. Papa Salvatore pointed onwards, and Symeon struggled out into an open yet darkened field.

He turned to look at the light spirit and said, 'It's still dark. I thought it would be different.'

Papa Salvatore's pulsating form stood at the edge of the cloud unmoving but eventually he raised first an arm and then uncurled a finger, pointing upwards. Symeon raised his head to follow the finger and exclaimed in wonder. He saw a canopy of stars of varying intensities. They twinkled peacefully and joyously above his head. 'No need to look down anymore' said Papa Salvatore."

#

Downstairs, Simon's mum Angela was in the kitchen making a cup of tea when the phone started ringing. She came back through to the living room, pressed the mute button on the telly, placed the hot cup on the side table and picked up her phone. The display said 'Carla' followed by an Italian telephone number. Angela accepted the call and sat down on the couch.

"Hi Carla," she said, "We seem to be talking a lot more these days. How are you?"

"Hi Angela," came Carla's accented voice, "Oh you know, getting by. How is Simon?"

"I was just about to pop up and see him, but you know, surprisingly he seems to be much better since he arrived home last week. I must admit it's been tough Carla, and it broke my heart to hear his screams in the night. But thankfully his arm is recovering, the blistering has calmed down and mercifully he is starting to sleep again. I don't know what changed. He had an appointment with the psychologist a few days ago and she said I should expect this to go on for months. Unusually, the last two or three nights he has gone to bed more easily – almost like he is looking forward to it."

"I'm pleased." Carla replied. "He has gone through such a lot. You know, the police in Bologna told me the fire started on the ground floor in an old lady's apartment. Apparently, it was caused by a faulty phone charger and that set light to some papers. They said the fire caught quickly and spread upwards to the other apartments. I still can't work out how Simon got the idea to cover himself in that wet towel and crouch down to crawl under the smoke."

Simon's mum sighed, "And poor Matteo. First time his son visits him back in Italy since our divorce and this happens. He was a good man."

"Yes, we will miss him dreadfully," replied Carla. "I keep thinking there should be someone to blame. Simon loses his father in a horrible way and it's all down to a stupid faulty plug".

Back upstairs, Simon was asleep, his bandaged arm resting on the top of the duvet. He was breathing softly, dreaming and thinking about his dad. At the door hovered the outline of a grey figure wearing a silver-grey cloak.